The Three Ys Men

The Three Ys Men

by

Joseph Pearce

The Saint Austin Press
1998

THE SAINT AUSTIN PRESS
296 Brockley Road
London   SE4 2RA
Tel   +44 (0) 181 692 6009
Fax +44 (0) 181 469 3609

Email: st_austin@compuserve.com
http://www.saintaustin.org

© 1998, Joseph Pearce

This book is sold subject to the condition that it shall not, by way of trade or otherwise, be lent, re-sold, hired out or otherwise circulated without the publisher's prior consent in any form of binding or cover other than that in which it is published and without a similar condition including this condition being imposed on the subsequent purchaser.

All rights reserved. No part of this publication may be reproduced or transmitted in any form or by any means, electronic or mechanical including photocopying, recording or any information storage or retrieval system, without prior permission in writing from the publishers.

A catalogue record for this book is available from the British Library.

ISBN 1 901157 02 4

For A.F.W. Simmonds
In gratitude

Foreword

I made the journey recounted in this book over four days in 1996 - on foot, which is the only way to make such a journey. The places visited en route are real places, described as they appeared to me on the days I arrived. Although the places remain, the days are no more, except as treasures enshrined in my memory.

But what of the Three Ys Men: Yore, the Ghost of Sussex Past; Yo!, the Ghost of Sussex Present; and Yet, the Ghost of Sussex Future? Are they real in the same sense?

Perhaps not in the same sense but in a true sense none the less and, what is more, they certainly seemed to *make* sense.

They came to me and the vision of them, their arguments and their adventures, allowed me to see life itself more clearly. With their help I seemed to see beyond the peripheral to the perennial, leaving behind the daily problems of existence to consider the primary problem of existence itself. They also showed me that even the most serious things need not be taken too seriously - or at least that they need not be taken too sombrely. For the Three Ys Men philosophy was not only fun but funny, and life was not only a process but an adventure - a wild adventure full of what Chesterton called 'the glorious gift of the senses and the sensational experience of sensation'.

When I reached the end of my journey they left me as suddenly as they had come to me and now they only remain as dim shadows. Ghosts who are ghosts of their former selves. Yore was, and I believe he still is, though where he is remains a mystery. Yo! certainly is, even though he wasn't and I often wish that he isn't. Yet is an enigma who wasn't and isn't, and exactly what he is or isn't remains to be seen.

Now that they are gone I sometimes wonder what they would have thought of my efforts to recount my journey with them. Perhaps Yore would have perceived the influence of Thomas Aquinas, Chesterton, and perhaps even Dickens, in the telling of the tale. He would have certainly seen similarities with *The Four Men*, a book he knew better than anyone. Yo! may have seen visions of Terry Pratchett lost in *Sophie's World* with Umberto Eco, and Yet would have informed me that he didn't read books and would wait for it to come out on a virtual reality video.

Either way, and whether or not I have succeeded, the following is an effort to go boldly where few have gone before. It is a voyage in transcience-fiction, beyond scientific fact or fantasy to transcientific truth. As such, it is a true story even if it strays from a strict rendition of the facts. It is also, above all, a mystery story because life is a mystery, truth is a mystery and reality is a mystery.

Returning to Chesterton, as I do often, he once remarked plaintively that we want truth, not facts, a view echoed by Tolkien and C. S. Lewis. All three saw the power of myth as a conveyer of truth. For my part, I am happy to follow humbly in their footsteps and offer this book to their memory.

Speaking on the socio-political level, Chesterton once remarked that evolution is what happens when everyone is asleep and revolution is what happens when everyone is awake. For once I am not sure that I agree with the great man, but speaking on the metaphysical level a similar analogy can be drawn. Surrealism is the dream; realism is the night; mysterealism is the dawn.

I invite those adventurous enough to follow in the footsteps of the three Ys men, to accompany me on the journey. It is possible that you will awake from the dream, step out from the night and disappear into the sunrise.

The Nineteenth of April, 1996

I was in Robertsbridge.
Why I was in Robertsbridge I couldn't really say. It had been a whim that I should go there. A spur-of-the-moment decision.
    Earlier that evening I had been in London amidst the maddening crowds. I had time to kill but no clear idea how to kill it. Absently I had followed the flow of homeward commuters over London Bridge. To my right I saw the glow of the sun setting a halo around the dome of St Paul's. To my left the magnificence of Tower Bridge sat astride the Thames. To its left the Tower of London nestled shyly between its larger neighbours, a timely reminder of the triumph of Mammon over the Medieval. Beyond it in the distance the Canaanite colossus of Canary Wharf winked at me.
    Following the flow I had found myself at London Bridge station. It was Friday evening. Drunks staggered and slurred, clown-like in the incongruity of collar-and-tied incoordination.
    "That's unreal!" A jacketed jester gesticulated, can-in-hand, as he passed.
    "Unreal!" agreed his colleague as they lurched away.
    It was a scene so typical of the late twentieth century. A *fin de siecle* fantasy. Yet it was no fantasy. What I was witnessing was a fact. But artificial. A fact too artificial to be real. I smiled at the apparent contradiction. Unreal!
    Unreal? Surreal certainly. It was at that moment that I had a sudden urge to escape, an irresistible compulsion to get away from this mass of humanity enduring existence on an artificial-life support machine. I would get real. I smiled again at my use of the modern idiotic idiom. I hated that particular phrase. Get real. It was meaningless. How could one possibly get unreal? Then I smiled again. Come to think of it, most of the modern world seemed to have

succeeded in getting extremely unreal. Either way, I was resolved to get real.

But how?

It was then that a human voice entered my consciousness. It was not a real human voice, but an artificial one. The taped voice of an announcer running through the destinations of the next train due at the platform onto which I'd strayed. One of the words struck home. Robertsbridge. I had heard of Robertsbridge. Yes, I remembered. One of my heroes had lived there for many years before his recent death. I had never met him. He had never even heard of me. But he was still a hero. He was more than a hero. He was a friend. A soul mate. I had read his books and in them he had spoken to me in ways that few writers had. I remembered a photograph on the back cover of one of his books. It showed him seated in front of the village sign at Robertsbridge.

Robertsbridge was real. I would go there.

Two hours later, seated in the George in Robertsbridge, I felt a great sense of disappointment. A television droned drivel in the corner, unwatched but seemingly omniscient. Lights flashed incessantly from a machine, unplayed but seemingly omnipresent. Worse still, the pub had no beer. Or at least the pub had no beer worthy of the name. I was drinking cider. Yet even that was barely worthy of the name. It was one of the mass-produced ciders, pumped with gas and emptied of flavour, which is sold all over the country to people who have never tasted real scrumpy. And this in a pub on the very edge of Kent, the former garden of England where hundreds of apple orchards once graced the countryside. Meandering into melancholy, I mused over the world into which I was exiled. I did not belong in an asylum where it was deemed uneconomic to sell locally produced cider in the local pub, or where it was cheaper to import apples from France than to pick them from the local trees. My reflections on a rotten apple led me to a *reductio ad absurdum*. If Robertsbridge was as unreal as London, everywhere was unreal. Reality was a myth.

"Heresy! Outright heresy. And, as with all heresy, utter nonsense!"

I sat up startled. The voice had come from nowhere. Looking around, I could see nobody nearby and the few people in the bar were all engrossed in private conversation. I looked down in utter bewilderment at the chemical fizz in the glass in front of me. Was I losing my sanity? Looking up again, I was astonished to find an old man sitting opposite, dressed in a suit of black broadcloth. He was thickset, had a furrowed brow and a salient chin, the prominence of which helped to disguise the flabbiness of his face. His features were fierce, intensifying the fear aroused by his uncanny arrival.

"Heresy, I say." His eyes pierced mine inquisitorially.

"I don't understand."

I was painfully aware of the inadequacy of my reply but I felt instinctively that the figure expected a response. In any case, the words were succinctly accurate. I didn't understand.

"No, you don't. A triangle has three sides. A square has four sides. A triangle is not a square. Reality is *not* a myth."

Listening to the stranger's bombastic dogmatism, I found my initial fear give way to anger. I was stung into an instant riposte: "Your comparison is simplistic and unfair. Geometry can be objectively demonstrated, whereas reality can only be subjectively experienced."

"More heresy! More nonsense!"

"Why?"

"Because the fact that those subject to reality can only perceive it subjectively does not negate the existence of the objective reality to which they are subject. On the contrary, the subject proves the existence of the object."

I was not sure that I agreed. I was not sure that I understood. But I felt it advisable to change the subject.

"Who are you?"

The stranger smiled and there was something in the genuine warmth of his countenance that mellowed my attitude. His reply, however, beggared belief: "I am the Ghost of Sussex Past."

"What!" I exclaimed incredulously.

"I am the Ghost of Sussex Past. At least, that is my full title. Or rather that is my full title in Sufferance. I had a different title in Militance and, hopefully, I shall have a newer and better title in Triumph."

"What on earth are you talking about?"

"It's not just on earth that I am talking about. Or rather, it is just on earth that I am talking about. Absolutely just. That's just it!"

"Pardon? If you're not prepared to speak the Queen's English there's no point in continuing because I can't understand a word you're talking about."

"But I am speaking the Queen's English."

"Which Queen? Queen Elizabeth the First? The Queen of Sheba? Your turn of phrase is so archaic that it certainly isn't current English."

"The Queen of whom I speak, and whose English I speak, will never be archaic."

"You are talking in riddles," I exclaimed in exasperation. "It is you who is speaking nonsense, not I?" The stranger smiled again: "Make up your mind. Am I speaking in riddles or am I speaking nonsense? I cannot be doing both. A riddle must make sense. Nonsense must not. We have come full circle. Now, where were we? Oh yes, a triangle has three sides. A square has four sides. A triangle is not a square. A riddle must make sense. Nonsense must not make sense. A riddle is not nonsense. Neither is nonsense a riddle. And, most important of all, reality is *not* a myth."

He laughed heartily and it suddenly dawned on me that the stranger was merely having fun. I didn't understand the nature or purpose of the game or, for that matter, whether it made sense or nonsense. Neither did I care. I was simply relieved that the ice had been broken.

I smiled: "Okay, you win. If you say you are the Ghost of Sussex Past, that's fine by me. Why not? It's a free country."

"Heresy! It is *not* a free country! You are a free man and I am a free man, but that has nothing to do with the country, and still less to do with the government of the country."

"Fine," I said, not wishing to take off on another bewildering tangent.

Once more, the stranger smiled.

"I'm sorry," he said. "I have the most annoying habit of playing with words - or, rather, of playing with the meaning of words. You see, I am a radical. Not the sort of radical you hear about today. Heavens, no. I am a radical in the radical sense of the word. I go back to the roots of a word to find its true meaning. It's fun, but it's also very enlightening. You'd be amazed how much nonsense is spoken because people have lost the meaning of the words they use or abuse."

"Well, I'm glad that you are interested in words because you certainly use enough of them!" The stranger laughed again, so enthusiastically that the ample protrusion of his stomach shook in a girthquake of pleasure. He always seemed to be laughing, obviously enjoying the sound of his own voice. Predictably enough, he continued: "Actually, what caused the initial confusion was not the archaic nature of my turn of phrase, but its ambiguity. When you asked me what on earth I was talking about, I replied that it was not *just* on earth that I am talking when I should have said it was not *only* on earth. Unfortunately, I cannot resist a pun when it presents itself - much to the annoyance of my friends who have to suffer my punning. Punishment I call it."

He laughed again and I began to despair of the conversation ever getting anywhere. Although I had known the stranger for only a few minutes, and although I still didn't know his true name, I was already in complete sympathy with his friends, whoever they may be. I too was dreading the next pun and the next deviation from the subject at hand. I made one last effort to get the dialogue back on course.

"You were about to tell me your name."

"I have already told you. Now, as I was saying, I should have said it was not *only* on earth instead of not *just* on earth. And when I say 'not only on earth' I mean that I am speaking of things that are not confined by nature, not natural."

"Not natural?" I enquired resignedly, attempting to stifle a sigh or a yawn.

"Yes, not natural. Not unnatural, you understand, but not natural."

This time I failed completely to stifle the yawn.

"Go on" I said, unconvincingly.

"I mean that it is beyond nature. It is beyond the natural. It transcends the natural. In short, it is supernatural."

"Supernatural?"

"Precisely. My name in Militance was what you would call the combination of my Christian name and my surname. Under that name I was quite well known in these parts since Sussex was my home. Now that I am dead, at least in the worldly and limited sense of the word, I find that particular name of no consequence."

"Now that you are dead . . ." I said, repeating the most interesting part of the sentence.

"Yes. Now that I am dead I prefer to use the name given me in Sufferance until He Who Names Everything gives me my final name in Triumph. My name, for the time being, that is, you undertand, until time is no longer being, is the Ghost of Sussex Past."

"The Ghost of Sussex Past . . ." I repeated, delving into his eyes for any obvious signs of lunacy.

"Yes" he said, "but as that is a bit of a mouthful you may call me Yore."

"Yore" I mumbled, unable to detect the signs of madness but determined none the less to humour the madman.

"Yes, Yore" repeated the madman, smiling unassumingly across the table at me.

As I gazed at him, it became clear that he was completely weird. His clothes, which at first I thought simply strange, suddenly took on a more menacing look. The black broadcloth suit gave him the appearance of a mourner from the turn of the century. He looked as though he could have stepped out of an old photograph, a coffin on his shoulders. Worse, he looked as if he could have stepped out of a coffin himself. The thought gave me the creeps. I had to make my escape.

"Well, it's been good talking to you, but I really must go to bed."

"Ah, sleep, I remember it well."

"Quite, now if you'll excuse me . . ."

"Certainly," the psychopath beamed, "I'll see you in the morning."

Not if I see you first, you won't. The thoughts remained unspoken but the loony smiled again as if he had heard every word.

I got up from the table and collected the key to my room from the landlord of the pub. I was relieved that I had booked a room in the George and that I didn't have to step out into the night with the madman. Before ascending the stairs I glanced back furtively to where he had been sitting. He had gone.

The Twentieth of April, 1996

I had a restless night. Visions of the self-styled "Ghost" of Robertsbridge haunted me. Not literally, obviously. I no more believed the crank to be a ghost than I believed my own mother to be a goat. I chuckled in the darkness of my room, remembering the bizarre conversation we'd had. The question was whether *he* believed he was a ghost. Or, to put it another way, was he a madman suffering delusions, or simply an eccentric with the strangest sense of humour imaginable?

It began to get light. The village clock struck. I counted the chimes. One . . . two . . . three . . . four . . . five . . . six. Six o'clock. I grunted. I was happy to believe that the clock, enthroned on a tower outside my bedroom window, added something to the character of the village. I was even content to accept that the chimes had a charm of their own - during daylight hours. At night they were an insomniac's curse. Certainly, this insomniac cursed. Couldn't they turn the thing off at midnight and switch it back on at eight in the morning? Obviously they couldn't stop the clock but they could at least stop the chimes. Why was it that they could put a man on the moon but they couldn't stop a clock chiming? Throughout the night, I'd learned to despise that clock. It was the clock's fault that I couldn't sleep. It had struck midnight. It had struck one. Then two, three, four, five and six. I hated it every hour, on the hour. I hated it as regular as clockwork. I grinned. Was it possible to hate something as regularly as clockwork? Of course it was. My relationship with the clock proved it.

Time passed. Nothing happened. Prostrate on my bed, I watched the light change on the ceiling. Morning had broken. Chimes shattered the silence. One . . . two . . . three . . . four . . . five . . . six . . . seven. Seven o'clock. Breakfast was at eight-thirty. I would get up at eight. I felt tired. No fear of oversleeping. The village alarm clock was set. Set to explode at eight o'clock. I dozed. Only lightly.

Occasionally I looked at the clock beside the bed. A quarter to eight. I turned over for a final snooze. Minutes passed. I waited for the chimes. Any moment now. Nothing. Soon. Time for another couple of minutes.

I awoke to the sound of a blackbird outside my window. What was the time? My God! Twenty past eight! What had happened to the deafening clang of the clock? It had gone off every hour throughout the night and then failed to chime on the one occasion I relied on it! I cursed that clock. For a moment I had the feeling that it had played a practical joke on me. Outwitted by a village clock. That must make me the village idiot! Smiling, I put the notion out of my mind. Inanimate objects simply didn't play jokes. No sense of humour. The thought cheered me up and I sprang into action. Ten minutes to breakfast.

Over breakfast I asked the landlord whether he was aware that the clock had failed to strike at eight o'clock. He smiled and said that he never noticed the clock chiming because he was so used to it. I envied him. He then offered a perfectly rational explanation for its failure. There was a man in the village who was responsible for winding it up. He had probably forgotten. I couldn't help wishing that he had forgotten eight hours earlier.

Paying the bill and saying goodbye, I stepped from the pub. It was a beautiful sunny day. More like July than April. The sun warmed my spirits as well as my body and I felt contented. I even felt rested, in spite of my lack of peace the previous night. I looked at the clock which was basking in the morning sunlight. "Good morning clock" I said out loud, aware that nobody was around. "I forgive you and I absolve you from your sin."

The clock didn't reply.

Suddenly I became aware that the clock and I had something in common. We both had time on our hands. On a day like today it would be a crime to return to the mechanical mayhem of London. And in any case there was no need. I had time to spare and I would use it to extend the

THE THREE YS MEN

duration of my escape. I would walk. Yes, that's it, I would walk. Where? Did it matter? How far? As far as I liked. In which direction? In the direction I was facing.

I strolled out purposefully, saluting the village clock as I passed. Almost immediately I was stopped in my tracks by the sound of a famliar voice.

"Good morrow! It's a beautiful morning, isn't it?"

Like the clock I was dumbstruck. I knew that voice. It was the madman. I squinted my eyes in the morning sun but I couldn't see him. Where was he? My vision cleared and there he was, seated at the base of the clock. A feeling of *deja vu* gripped me. I had been here before. No, of course I hadn't. I had never been to Robertsbridge before in my life. Wait a moment. I know why the scene appeared so familiar. The loony was sitting in exactly the same place and in exactly the same pose as that struck by the hero on the back of my book. Exactly the same. It was uncanny. There he sat, smiling, his chin resting on top of his walking stick. Yet it wasn't the hero. The madman didn't look anything like him. The hero had been slim, the madman was decidedly stout. The hero had a kind, broad smile, the madman, though smiling, looked stern. The hero had been totally bald on top, the madman, though receding, still had a good head of hair. No, the madman looked nothing like the hero. And, in any case, the hero had been dead for nearly six years.

"And I've been dead for much longer than that" said the madman, reading my thoughts.

"How did you know what I was thinking?" I stuttered.

"My ears are not as your ears" he said simply.

"Who *are* you?" I urged, aware that the stranger was even stranger than I had originally thought.

"Stranger stranger. I like that! You're learning!"

He had done it again. Even my thoughts weren't safe from this man, if indeed he was a man and not a ghost as he claimed.

"I am both" he said, "the two are not mutually

exclusive."

"Pardon?"

"Man and ghost. They are not mutually exclusive. I am both. A man. And a ghost."

I made no reply. How does one reply to a statement like that?

He continued: "And while I'm about it, although I am indeed a man, I am not a madman. Nor am I a loony, or a crank, or a nutter, or a psychopath, or any of the other labels you've seen fit to attach to me. It's hardly my fault that I am dead. We are all dead in the end. Being dead doesn't make one mad. Quite the contrary. Sanity in the objective and absolute sense is only fulfilled *after* death."

No reply.

"Please address me by my correct name. Yore at your service."

He held out his hand in friendship. Rather hesitantly I took it and was somewhat relieved to find that I was grasping solid, warm flesh and blood.

"Incidentally," he added, smiling, "when I say Yore at your service, I mean Yore at your service and not you're at your service. Do I make myself clear?"

"Hardly" I replied, "but I think I know what you mean."

"In any case, you are about to go for a walk and I am going to come with you. Indeed, I am to be your guide."

"Now hold on for a minute" I protested.

"By all means, I have all the time in the world, and more."

"Well I don't. I have a week to myself and that's the way I'd like to keep it."

"Listen. I have been sent to guide you. It's my duty. But not only a duty. It will be a pleasure to show you the beauty of my county. There is so much to see."

"And I am perfectly capable of seeing it alone."

"On the contrary, you are totally incapable of seeing it alone. For instance, where exactly were you headed when I introduced myself just now?"

"Oh, I don't know. Somewhere. Anywhere. Does it matter?"

"Somewhere and anywhere don't exist. They are not on the map. And yes it does matter."

"Why?"

"Because if it didn't matter it wouldn't be worth doing."

"Why?"

For an instant Yore looked puzzled and I rejoiced at what I perceived to be a point scored in a game of oneupmanship.

"In any case" he continued, changing the subject. "Do you know exactly in which direction you were headed?"

"Does it matter?" I repeated, enjoying the exchange and looking to score another point.

"Yes, yes, yes!" Yore exclaimed emphatically. "You were heading in a direction that leads to . . ."

His voice trailed off as if he were afraid to utter the word.

I waited.

"Yes?" I urged, intrigued.

He whispered something inaudible.

"What was that?"

He whispered the dreaded word again, but still too low to hear.

"You'll have to speak up, I can't hear you."

"You were heading towards . . . Kent."

He seemed embarrassed at having said the four-letter word.

I laughed: "What? What's so terrible about Kent."

"Keep your voice down" he whispered, "someone might hear you."

"Preposterous!" I exclaimed and started to stroll off in the direction of the dreaded place.

"No! Wait!"

He strode after me with a speed and agility that belied

his age.

"You wanted to escape from the cares of the world, but you won't do it there. It's impossible. It's full of hideous places like Maidstone, Sevenoaks, Bexley and Gravesend. Urgh! Gravesend. What an appropriately named town. If the grave's end were really as bad as that I'd commit suicide. But then it's a bit late for me to do that isn't it? And, in any case, suicide's a sin. *He* wouldn't like it."

He paused for a moment, crossed himself, mumbled a prayer, then continued.

"My God! You may even end up in Dartford!"

That was it. I broke down with laughter.

"You win! Take me to your leader."

"I can't do that, you're not dead yet."

I shook my head in disbelief. I was in for a crazy couple of days.

We did an about-face and walked back towards the George. Passing the pub and the few houses which lined the road beyond it, we reached a small lane which led down to, and under, the railway line. It was not until we had left the road and were walking along a quiet track, leading uphill, that Yore spoke again.

"Isn't this beautiful? I had almost forgotten exactly how beautiful it is."

I agreed wholeheartedly, rejoicing in the tranquility of my surroundings. It was lambing season and dozens of new-born lambs gambolled enthusiastically in the field to our right while their mothers munched indifferently.

Yore continued: "We shall follow in my own footsteps. Many years ago when I was still alive, at the very start of this present century, I set out to walk the entire length of my county. I started from Robertsbridge and was determined to pay homage to the glory of Sussex by walking with her for as far as she would go. Believe me, you could not have a better guide than I to her secret places. I know every inch of her. Mind you, we may not take exactly the same route that I took then. Heavens, no.

Parts of Sussex have succumbed to the new religions and we cannot go where these have taken root, or should I say rootlessness because the new religions have no roots. They hate roots and glory in the destruction of roots. They are like a fungus that feeds on the roots of their forefathers until those roots are rotten and poisoned."

He looked not only solemn but sombre as he spoke these words. As he finished he sank into a deep, thought-filled silence. I wanted to know more.

"What do you mean by new religions? I know of no new religions in England. A few sects maybe but nothing worthy of note."

"It is a new paganism. They have turned their back on God and have started to worship the godgets."

"Godgets?"

"Yes, all different sorts of godgets. They are not particularly loyal to any particular godget for very long. Every now and then a new godget comes along and they drop the old godget they had been worshipping and pay homage to the latest godget. At least until the next one comes along. It is a restless religion. The worst of the godgets is the inferno. Everywhere the inferno is worshipped there is destruction. The worship of the inferno has laid much of my county to waste."

Again he sank into a wistful silence. But again I refused to leave him be, puzzled at these latest riddles.

"What are infernos?"

"Infernos are the godgets powered by the infernal combustion engine. They are everywhere. They are all powerful. Omnipresent and omnipotent. Alfa and Romeo. The beginning of the end."

He was silent again for a moment. Then he put his hand on my shoulder.

"Come, I am being unnecessarily pessimistic. Things are not as bad as all that. I know a secret way through my county where the godgets and the infernos have not penetrated."

His spirits seemed to lift and he lengthened his stride. I followed as we passed through a farm with goats tethered in the yard. We strode further uphill past an old moat until he stopped at the brow of a hill. Spread out in front of us was a wonderful, undulating view. Below us, about half a mile ahead, was a huge expanse of water. Beyond and above it was a large wood, deciduous on the far banks of the water but coniferous towards the top of the hill behind.

"It's beautiful" I said.

"Darwell Reservoir. Yes, it is beautiful. And necessary, I dare say. Of course, I remember the valley before the man-made deluge. That was beautiful too."

We strolled on more slowly now, taking in the view before us as we passed downhill towards the water. Above, a lone lark serenaded us, unseen but unmistakable. I scoured the sky for a sign of where the sound was coming from, straining unsuccessfully for a sight of the songstress. In the end I was content that the lark should be the opposite of Victorian children, heard but not seen.

Eventually we reached a small road where the sighting of a car was as rare as the sighting of a lark. We followed it for a couple of miles in blissful silence, the only sound being the rustling of shrews or mice in the soft verges to either side. Like the larks they were also heard but never seen. However, we did sight a nuthatch scampering rodent-like up the side of a tree, and a weasel who, for a few seconds, seemed as intrigued by us as we were of it. Its black eyes gazed at us, neck straining for a better view, before the novelty wore off and it scurried for cover.

"This is so peaceful" I said, wishing to give voice to my thoughts. "And I don't believe that I have ever seen so much wildlife in so short a space of time."

"A lot can happen in a short space of time. It is only a short space of time since I last did this walk. It was 1902 to be precise. In those days, when I walked the Sussex weald, I would see polecats and pine martens, black rats and red squirrels. They are all gone from Sussex now. And the mouse-eared bat hasn't been spotted for several years. Missing, presumed dead."

We strolled on until we had left Darwell Reservoir behind us and had passed through the outer fringes of Darwell Wood. As we approached the village of Hollingrove I spotted a large tower on top of the hill ahead.

"Is that the ruins of an old castle?"

"Hardly," Yore replied. "It's the ruins of a new folly. Well newish. It was built nearly two hundred years ago."

"Why?"

"To see the ruins of an old castle."

"What?"

"I see you know nothing of Honest Jack Fuller. A giant among men. A true Son of Sussex. That fine structure you see ahead is Honest Jack's Tower. There is a story behind it and I shall tell it. During the 1820's Bodiam Castle, which had been built on the easternmost edge of the county to keep the wicked men of Kent at bay, was threatened with destruction. Years of neglect had taken its toll and a firm of Hastings builders had gained permission to demolish it. It was then that Honest Jack rescued this priceless relic of our Sussex civilisation. He bought Bodiam Castle for the sum of £3,000. Furthermore, he set about repairing the Postern Tower and set up new oaken gates at the entrance. Now, Honest Jack's Tower was built so that Squire Fuller could direct operations without having to leave his estate. Bodiam Castle can be seen from the top of the Tower and Honest Jack watched the progress of the work through a telescope. The workmen, for their part, were able to signal to the Tower for materials. The Tower, therefore, is a shrine to the conservation of my county's heritage."

While Yore was eulogising, we had passed through the quiet hamlet of Hollingrove and had walked up the hill beyond. As he finished, we were standing at the base of the Tower.

"Shall we go in?" I asked, doing so before waiting for an answer.

Yore followed me through the arched entrance.

"It's changed. The original wooden staircase is no longer here."

"Shall we go up?" I asked, starting to climb the iron staircase which had obviously been installed to replace the wooden one.

"Excellent!" I exclaimed. "The view from here is brilliant!"

Yore was evidently pleased with my enthusiasm for his county. He set about describing the panorama.

"Back there," he said, pointing east, "is Robertsbridge from whence we started. It derived its name from Robert de St Martin who founded a Cistercian abbey there in 1176. Sadly for Sussex, Robertsbridge Abbey is no longer standing. What remains of it forms part of a local farm. To the south west," he continued, turning and pointing towards a domed building on the side of a hill, "is Honest Jack's Temple. It was built for Squire Fuller in the Grecian style by Sir Robert Smirke. No doubt you know Sir Robert as the architect responsible for many of London's finest buildings, including the British Museum, Somerset House, the Royal Mint and the Covent Garden Theatre."

In truth, I had never even heard of Sir Robert Smirke but I decided to keep my ignorance to myself. It was then I remembered that my companion could hear my thoughts as readily as he could hear my words. I felt ashamed of my dishonesty but Yore tactfully passed over my philistinism and continued.

"About a mile beyond the Temple, on the summit of the next hill, is the Sugar Loaf, another of Honest Jack's creations - and my favourite. Certainly, it doesn't compare architecturally with the Temple and poor Sir Robert hates it so much. Everytime anybody thinks that he had anything to do with its design and construction he turns in his grave. He never manages to rest in peace. The poor fellow is constantly turning and has worn a hole in his coffin through the constant agitation. At any rate, he shall not be turning on my account. Sir Robert Smirke had *nothing* to do with the Sugar Loaf. Sleep well Bob. Any how, and in spite of its architectural limitations, it is still my favourite and I shall tell you why. It is said that Honest Jack made a wager while away in London claiming he could see the spire of St Giles Church in Dallington from his estate. On his return he found this to be untrue and to win the wager he had the Sugar Loaf erected in one night. As a result the structure is weak and has been described as nothing more than stones held together by mud. Nonetheless, it does look remarkably similar to the spire of Dallington Church - at least from a distance. I know this is a case of Honest Jack failing to live up to his name, but have you ever known an act of dishonesty carried out in such style!"

Taking one last look eastward along the valley back to Robertsbridge, and taking a certain pleasure in being able to see, spread before us, the ground we'd covered that morning, we descended the stairs. From the Tower it was a short walk across fields to Brightling village. As we approached the church, with Brightling Park, the grounds of Squire Fuller's ancestral home on our left, I beheld one of the most bizarre sights I'd ever seen in an English village. There, in the churchyard, stood a huge pyramid, a full twenty-five feet high, about as in keeping as Ian Paisley at the Vatican.

"What on earth is that!"

"Ah," Yore replied, relishing the moment, "that is the Tomb of Honest Jack Fuller of Brightling!"

"Some gravestone!"

"Yes, it was designed by Sir Robert Smirke and is said to be based on the Tomb of Cestius in Rome. Honest Jack, a giant in life, was determined to be a giant in death. He had the tomb built in 1811, twenty-three years before he died. Furthermore, it is said that he was interred sitting at an iron table, a full meal before him, a bottle of claret at arm's length, dressed for dinner and wearing a top hat. The floor around him was strewn with broken glass so that when the Devil came to claim him he might at least cut his feet in the process. But I don't believe the Prince of Lies had any claim on Honest Jack. In spite of his follies and self-indulgent excesses, he was a good man at heart. The fact that he desired to be buried on hallowed ground in the churchyard alongside his people proves his good intent. Did you know that many of his peers tried to persuade him to be buried in the Temple on his own estate? He refused. Although it would doubtless have made a fine mausoleum he was too wise to be proud in death. The very fact that he had the tomb built twenty-four years before he died so that he could be reminded of his own mortality every time he looked out of his window towards the churchyard is ample proof of his humility. If further proof were needed, the choice of verse on the wall of the interior of the tomb should prove sufficient. It is the ninth verse of Thomas Gray's *Elegy in a Country Churchyard*:

> The boast of heraldry, the pomp of pow'r
> And all that beauty, all that wealth e'er gave
> Await alike th' inevitable hour
> The paths of glory lead but to the grave."

"This is too much! I have never heard so much rubbish in my whole life!"

The voice was not mine. Neither was it Yore's. We both looked around and then at each other. There was no visible sign of the source of the myterious voice. It spoke again.

"Old man, you distort the facts. You have turned Mad Jack Fuller into Saint Jack Fuller. It won't do. No, it won't do at all."

Following the direction of the voice, we both looked up. Perched precariously on the point of the pyramid sat a youth who appeared to be about eighteen years of age. A pair of trendy, ankle-length trainers adorned his feet, which, from the unusual angle at which we first saw him, were the nearest part of his anatomy. The furthest part, his head, was topped by an American baseball cap, worn back-to-front.

"Yo!" he exclaimed, smiling.

"Hi!" I responded.

"Not really," he replied, "about twenty-five feet."

"Very funny, are you some kind of comedian?"

"No, Yo!"

"Yo?"

"Yes, Yo!"

With that, the youth slid down the side of the pyramid with a speed which looked incredibly painful. Arriving at ground level, apparently none the worse for wear, he bowed, beamed, and held out his hand.

"Yo!"

"Yo!" I responded, shaking his hand vigorously.

"You too?" He replied, puzzled.

"Pardon?"

"Are you Yo! too?"

"Are you a Japanese tourist?" Yore quipped sardonically.

"No, Yo!" the youth insisted.

"Pardon?" I repeated, perplexed.

"Yo!. My name is Yo!"

"Oh! Yo!" I said, everything suddenly becoming clear. "Yo! Yo!"

Yore raised his eyes heavenwards and groaned. Then, by way of an afterthought which seemed to cheer him, he added: "Life certainly has its ups and downs."

"Of course," Yo! continued, "Yo! is not my real name. Real names are naff, don't you think?"

"No," Yore interjected, "naff names are naff. Real names are real."

Ignoring the interjection, Yo! continued.

"Yo! is my nickname. It has more street cred. My real name is a bit of a mouthful. The Ghost of Sussex Present. Yuk! No, I don't like my real name. It's embarrassing.

Please call me Yo!."

"Okay Yo!" I said cheerfully.

"Oh my God," mumbled Yore.

"Anyway," Yo! continued, "as I was saying, Mad Jack Fuller is not a suitable subject for canonisation."

"I never suggested for a moment that he was," Yore complained. "I was merely pointing out that he was a good man. A good man who has been much maligned and misunderstood. Not least by those who insist on calling him Mad."

"Well, he was mad! He was as eccentric as hell!"

"Hell is certainly eccentric if you mean that it is far from the true centre of things. But we are all eccentric, even if we are not quite as eccentric as hell. You, my dear Ghost of Sussex Present, are more eccentric than most."

"I am not!"

"I meant it as a compliment."

"I could do without those sort of back-handed compliments, thank you very much. And my name is Yo!"

Yore smiled mischievously.

"Of course, I know many who would come right out and call you mad. Incidentally, may I call you Present for short?"

"No you may not! My name is Yo!"

"Oh dear, I hope I am not making Present tense. I was merely trying to point out that there is a very important difference between eccentricity and madness. We are all, to one degree or other, eccentric. Whereas only some of us," he said, pausing to grin at Yo!, "only some of us are mad."

"Yes!" snapped Yo!, "and Mad Jack Fuller fits perfectly into both categories. Not only was he mad, wasting so much money on the building of frivolous follies, but he was an obnoxious reactionary who supported the slave trade from which he made most of his wealth."

"Much of his wealth, certainly," Yore replied thoughtfully. "But not all. Most of it came from the iron industry, and particularly from the foundry at Heathfield.

He did have slaves in Jamaica and it is a stain on his character that, in this one instance at least, he allowed self-interest to colour his judgment. Indeed, he was wrong about other things too. He was a rabid opponent of the old faith of Sussex, opposing the passage of the Bill which at last restored some of their ancient rights to England's beleaguered Catholics. Nonetheless, when all is said and done, I maintain that Honest Jack Fuller was a good man at heart. Furthermore, he had the courage to treat the House of Commons with the contempt it obviously deserves. On one occasion, during a heated debate, he had the temerity to call the Speaker an insignificant little man in a wig. In another debate, which was far from heated but, on the contrary, was decidedly dull, Honest Jack enlivened the proceedings by leaping to his feet and making the most impressive and important speech ever delivered to Parliament. Much to the dismay of the House, he told the assembled Members about Sussex and her glories and of the superiority of Sussex over all other parts of the Kingdom. Never before or since has the House of Commons been blessed with such a learned and wise discourse on matters of primary importance. But it was typical of the Members of that contemptible body that they didn't like the truth, even when expressed so eloquently. For several minutes, they cried in unison 'Order, Order' in an effort to silence Honest Jack's oration. But to no avail because he went on in his booming voice, regaling them with the virtues of his Sussex home. Then, quite finished, he walked out on that bemused assembly, leaving them to their London ways, and returned to Brightling."

"London's gain was Brightling's loss," asserted Yo! when Yore had finished delivering his homily. "Thereafter, disillusioned with Parliament, he wasted his money in a scandalous fashion on these follies which continue to deface the local landscape."

"Clearly your economics are as silly as your clothes," Yore parried. "You should know that the follies were an important source of employment locally. Not only were local craftsmen and labourers dependent for their employment on the building of these follies but he did much else to improve the lot of the people of Brightling. Do you see that wall over there? It's the wall surrounding Brightling Park, Honest Jack's estate, and it stretches for four miles around the grounds, varying in depth from four to six feet. Why do you think it was built?"

"To keep the peasants out of his grounds of course. Why else does anyone build a wall?"

"To keep the peasants out of the workhouse. It was built to provide work for the unemployed. Between 1815 and 1817, when the wall was built, unemployment was very high. Honest Jack laid out £10,000 to cover the cost of labour. And, my dear Sussex Present, in the more recent past, a little over ten years ago to be precise, Honest Jack's wall was again providing much needed employment. It was in a dilapidated condition and much in need of repair. Its renovation provided further employment to young people a century and a half after Squire Fuller's original job creation scheme. And while I'm about it, perhaps I should mention the lighthouse he had built on the cliffs at Beachy Head, or the lifeboat he presented to the people of Eastbourne, or the barrel organ in the church behind us, the largest in the whole of England, or the bells in the tower named after the six battles at which the Duke of . . ."

"Okay! Okay! We get the point. Perhaps old Squire Fuller wasn't as bad as I thought. If you ask me though, he still had a few screws loose."

Yore appeared to accept Yo!'s modified judgment and seemed happy to let the matter rest. The three of us then set out on the road heading west out of Brightling village. After about a mile, as Yore was holding forth about Squire Fuller's Observatory which surmounted a hill on our left, something much more interesting caught my eye.

"What's that?" I exclaimed.

"That," began Yore with evident enthusiasm, "is the

Brightling Needle".

"Hideous!" remarked Yo!

"Squire Fuller, I presume." I said, recognising all the hallmarks of another folly.

"Yes," resumed Yore, "it is sixty-five feet high and stands on the second highest point in Sussex. It was built by Honest Jack to celebrate Wellington's victory at Waterloo in 1815."

"But what's the point?" asked Yo! plaintively.

"That thing at the very top, sixty-five feet from the ground." Yore quipped, smiling. "If it didn't have a point it wouldn't be a Needle would it?"

"Very funny," replied Yo!, clearly unamused. "I mean, it serves no function. It has no utilitarian purpose. It makes no sense."

"On the contrary, it makes very good sense. The best sense in the world. It makes a sense of humour. It is another of Honest Jack's jokes. And bearing in mind the employment it provided, it is a very good practical joke also. Thank God for Honest Jack's sense of humour. It puts the bright into Brightling."

At that moment, the conversation was brought to a sudden halt by the sound of rumbling. It was coming from the other side of the hedge in the field in which the Needle stood. The rumbling grew louder and I thought we were witnessing the impossible, an earthquake in Sussex. In fact, what we were about to witness was infinitely more incredible than an earthquake. We peered in the direction of the noise and saw the earth begin to move in the field, swaying up and down as though the soil had become liquid. Then, with a gunky glug, a head emerged above ground level. It opened its eyes and scowled at us.

"Will you *please* keep your noise down. Some of us are trying to sleep."

I gazed agog and aghast. I had seen some weird things already but this was the most bizarre sight of all. Even Yore appeared lost for words at the sight of the apparition.

The figure had surfaced sufficiently so that most of it was now visible. It wore a glossy, one-piece suit, claret in colour, which clung to every crevice of its fat, asexual body. The garment, if indeed it was a garment, was so close-fitting that it almost appeared to be the creature's skin. It covered every inch, from the tips of its fingers to the top of its head. Only its face was uncovered. And what a strange face! Although it was larger than the face of a full-grown man it had the shape and features of a baby.

The baby started to cry.

"Oh, megamag-doubleplus-ungood!" it bawled, "this is terrible. I feel like death warmed up! I need a shot!"

Looking down, it pressed a small button attached to its wrist. Instantly its features lit up. A glazed expression followed. Then it changed colour from claret to a bright, garish electric blue.

"Megayards-powerplay! Weeeeeee!!!"

The creature, which had still been knee-deep in soil, took off like a hot air balloon and floated ecstatically round and round the Brightling Needle. Then it perched itself on tiptoe on the obelisk's point and pirouetted manically. Finally, it glided down towards us until it was a few yards away, floating about five feet from the ground.

"Cool!" exclaimed Yo! "How did you do that!"

"It's mega-simple. All you need is one of these," it replied, pointing to its wrist.

"What is it?"

"A magic button."

"Cool! Where can I get one."

"Avant garde! You can't. It hasn't been invented yet."

"Well, thank God for small mercies!" Yore remarked.

"Mega-avant-garde-powerplay-in-earnest! Don't be such a stick-in-the-mud!"

"It was you, and not I, who was stuck in the mud."

"Not any longer," the cherub chirped, "the magic button set me free."

"If that's what you call freedom, I thank God I'm free

from it."

"Magpie! What harm is there in the odd flight of fancy?"

"It was certainly an odd flight," I remarked.

The cherub smiled.

"Yards! Allow me to introduce myself. I am the Ghost of Sussex Future, sometimes referred to as Sussex Yet To Be. You may call me Yet."

"Yo! Yet!" said Yo! "I am Yo!"

"Yards! Yo!" said Yet.

"And I am I" said I.

"And you're . . ?" asked Yet expectantly.

"Correct." Yore replied tersely.

"And where are you going?" Yet continued.

"West."

"Mega-yards-powerplay! May I come with you? It would be doubleplus good to have some company for a few days."

"Certainly," I replied. "We are walking the entire length of Sussex."

"Walking? Avant. I can't walk."

"Then float along with us," I said cheerfully.

"Avant-garde. The effect of the magic button wears off too quickly if I float for too long."

"Well that settles it," Yore interjected. "If you can't walk we'll have to take our leave. Good day."

"Wait," said Yo! "I have an idea. Why don't I hang around here with Yet while the two of you carry on. To tell the truth, I hate walking. My feet are killing me, or at least they would be if it were possible for me to be killed. At any rate, they hurt like hell."

"I doubt it," replied Yore. "Hell hurts a lot more than your feet. What you need is a decent pair of boots. It's no wonder that your feet are hurting in those things."

"I wouldn't be seen dead in d.m.s! They're so uncool!"

"d.m.s?" asked Yore, puzzled.

"Doctor Martens," I said.

"What's the world coming to?" Yore exclaimed in exasperation. "Do they now only give out boots on prescription?"

"At any rate," said Yo!, ignoring Yore's ignorance, "I think I'll stay here with Yet. I'm not walking another metre."

"Yards!" said Yet.

"No, metres," said Yo!

"Metres are yards!" said Yet.

"Not exactly," murmered Yore.

"Not when you have to walk them," stated Yo! with a finality indicating that he had made up his mind not to go on.

"Well," I said, holding out my hand to Yo!, "I suppose that this is goodbye. It's been good to know you, even if it was for such a short time. But it would have been great if you could have come with us. You Yo! and you Yet. We would have made a fine company. A weird company, certainly, but a fine company also. Yore, Yo! and Yet - the three Ys. The three Ys men! Still, if it is not to be . . ."

"Hold on," said Yo! "I think you are forgetting who I am. As I am the Ghost of Sussex Present I can be present whenever I like. I'll be around as you pass through Sussex. After all, the county belongs to me now. It used to belong to Yore, but now it is mine. He left it to me."

"God help Sussex," muttered Yore.

"I'll just skip all the boring bits. The walking bits. It's such an old-fashioned way of getting around. Rest assured, I'll be seeing you and I'll bring Yet along with me. For the time being, I'd like to find out more about this magic button."

After bidding Yo! and Yet a fond farewell, I departed with Yore for pastures new. We left the road almost immediately and took a small farm track which led eventually to woodland. The woods sloped steeply to a small, secluded hamlet, situated on the banks of a fast-flowing stream. We then climbed up the far-side of the valley through Dallington Forest, emerging at Watkin's Down. Pressing on, we eventually arrived at the northern outskirts of Punnett's Town where a large and impressive windmill dominated the landscape, its brilliant white weather-boarded sides resplendent against the clear blue sky.

"Ah!" exclaimed Yore with an air of satisfaction, "Blackdown Mill."

He stood still for a few moments, drinking deep draughts of the view before him. Slowly, he approached.

"You know," he said, "this mill stands as a monument to renewal. It is living proof that there is life after death. For Blackdown Mill was dead, but now it lives. Its erection was a resurrection."

Even allowing for his hyperbole, I was intrigued. I asked him to explain.

"Well, I am a great admirer of windmills. And Sussex windmills are the best in the world. When I was alive in the worldly sense, I lived next to a fine old windmill at the other end of the county. I spent a great deal of time and effort restoring it. After I died in the worldly sense, the people of the village in which I lived named the mill after me. Although I have rejected the world and its vanities, I am flattered by the honour they bestowed on me. If I am remembered for nothing else in my previous life, I shall be happy that I am remembered for that."

Yore paused, overtaken by memories, and gazed absently into the distance. Returning to the present, he focused again on the structure in front of us.

"But this mill, Blackdown Mill, has a place of honour among all the mills of Sussex. Even my own mill in the west must pay homage. There has been a mill on this sight for over two hundred years. The previous one burned down in the middle of the nineteenth century and the one you see in front of you rose from the ashes. But in 1928 it became unworkable when the curb on the cap was damaged. Worse was to follow. The sails were removed. One was sold for thirty shillings, one was dismantled and the timber used for repairs on nearby buildings, and the other two were broken up for firewood. In 1934 the cap was removed and the machinery taken out. Soon all that remained was an empty, decaying shell, used as a store for cattle feed. That should have been the end of Blackdown Mill. It was dead and buried but, thanks to the efforts of one man, it didn't rest in pieces. Timber was hauled from the woods. It was cut and shaped and used in the rebuilding of the domed cap. An old windshaft was hoisted into position. New machinery was assembled, a fan was built and two pairs of stones installed. Finally, in 1974, all four sweeps were in position. Blackdown Mill had risen from the dead!"

Yore seemed lifted by the telling of the tale and even I was heartened by the way the mill had defied the winds of change.

"Come," he said, "let's drink to the health of Blackdown Mill. There is an inn half a mile down the road."

Needing no further encouragement, I followed him as he strode out purposefully in the direction of the inn.

We arrived at the Barley Mow and as we crossed the threshold a succession of sudden thoughts occurred to me. If Yore was a ghost, could anybody else see him or was I in the company of an invisible man? If so, conversation could prove a trifle embarrassing. Also, if Yore was a ghost, did he suffer from hunger and thirst? I was extremely hungry and thirsty, having had nothing to eat or drink since breakfast, but was my companion also in need of sustenance?

"Yes, no, yes and no."

Yore's succinct reply to each of my questions served as an instant reminder that my thoughts were not my own. He elaborated.

"Yes other people can see me. The Past is always

visible to those who have their eyes open. Therefore, no you are not in the company of an invisible man and you need not fear embarrassment. Yes, I do suffer from hunger and thirst, although it is not a hunger for food nor a thirst for drink. Therefore, no I am not in need of sustenance, at least not that sustenance linked to food and drink. As to that greater Sustenance I am as dependent on it for my existence as any other part of God's creation."

"I take it you don't want a drink then."

"Of course I want a drink!"

"But you just said . . ."

"I said I didn't *need* a drink. I never said I didn't *want* a drink. The enjoyment of the barley brew is one of life's legitimate pleasures. Heaven forbid that I should ever lose the taste for the nutbrown ale! A pint of the landlord's very best bitter, please, and a healthy serving of bread and cheese!"

I complied with his wishes, ordering the same for myself, and we sat down by the window at the rear of the inn and enjoyed the wide expanse of the weald spread before us.

As we sat there, I was puzzled by further thoughts. Yore answered them before being asked.

"Yes, Yo! is visible to the world at large. He was right when he said that he is always present. The present is ever-present. And it is visible, even when we wish that it wasn't. But as for Yet . . . He is another case completely. In fact, he is, in many ways, the opposite to Yo!. Unlike the present, the future is never visible - even when we wish that it was. People are always imagining what the future will be. But it is elusive. It always remains nothing but a figment of our imagination. When it arrives it is seldom as we imagined it. And, of course, by the time it arrives it is no longer the future."

"But we saw the future this afternoon."

"We saw something which said it was the future this afternoon."

"Are you saying that Yet was an impostor, a liar?"

"Possibly. Possibly not. Let's look at it laterally. I am no more able to see the future than are you or Yo!. None the less, I believe that I have a better idea of what Yet is to be. After all, I have been around long enough to see certain patterns emerging from out of the past. But to really know the future is a science known only to One. Indeed, it is not *a* science. It is *the* science. Omniscience."

"So who or what did we see this afternoon?"

"Ah, to be or Yet to be. That is the question!"

"Yes, but what is the answer?"

"No, Yet is the answer. It's just that we don't know Yet yet."

"This is all too much! Why are there always more questions than answers?"

"Heresy! There are not more questions than answers. There is an answer to every question. It's just that we don't know the answers. Indeed, as often as not we do not even know the questions."

"I give up!"

"But if you give up you'll never know the answers!"

I sighed resignedly: "The best answer at the moment is another pint of beer. Will you join me?"

Yore grinned: "Is the Pope a Catholic?"

Happy that he had finished with a question to which we both knew the answer, I ordered two more drinks.

Half an hour later, we emerged once more into the sunlight and continued our westward trek. Within an hour, we had passed through Old Heathfield and were skirting Heathfield Park to the south. Our intention, Yore explained, was to avoid new Heathfield which had changed beyond recognition since he was last there.

It was then we beheld a stranger ahead. He was young, about eighteen, and he was dressed like a designer rebel. His bleached hair contrasted starkly with his black eyebrows. He wore a black leather jacket, studded and decorated with the satanic-sounding name of some rock group. Skin-tight jeans hugged his thighs and black doctor marten boots adorned his feet. He was the archetypal self-conscious stereotype. The original rebel without a clue. Or, since he was identical in all respects to millions of others around the world, the very unoriginal rebel without a clue.

"Yo!" He shouted as we approached.

It can't be, I thought.

"But it is," said Yore.

"What on earth are you doing dressed like that," I asked as we approached.

"Do you like it? It's cool isn't it?"

"Cool?" said Yore, incredulously. "In weather like this? You must be boiling alive!"

"What would you know, old man?" Yo! retorted. "It's hip. Heavy metal."

"Heavy what?"

"Heavy metal."

"What? Gold? Lead? Mercury?"

"Freddy Mercury! Get a life! He's not heavy metal. Black Sabbath, Iron Maiden and Motorhead. *That's* heavy metal!"

"Really? The first is quintessentially evil, the second is a barbaric way of murdering someone, but the third seems to sum up the lump of barely-functioning matter which sits on your shoulders. As to getting a life, I have one already thank you."

While Yore and Yo! were going hammer and tongs over matters metallic, I found myself staring at Yo!'s feet.

"Doctor martens?" I asked, during a lull in their discussion.

"Yeah, cool aren't they?"

"But you said you wouldn't be seen dead in doctor martens."

"Did I? Oh well, they're the thing to be seen in now. The height of fashion."

"One should be wary of the heights of fashion," said Yore. "It's a long way down when one falls from them.

Now, take the case of the Green Man of Brighton."

"The Green Man of Brighton!" Yo! scoffed. "What new fable is this?"

"It's no fable. But a fact. Though one could call it a parable since there is a lesson to be learned from it."

"Go on," I said, as willing as ever to hear a good story.

Yo! grunted in disapproval but sat submissively as Yore began.

"The Green Man of Brighton was a dedicated follower of fashion. He had sartorial elegance off to a fine art. His real name, in case you think I'm inventing the whole story, was Henry Cope, though everyone knew him as the Green Man. The reason, if you haven't guessed, was because his choice of colour was green. Green pantaloons, green waistcoat, green frock coat, green cravat. And that was not all. He ate nothing but green fruits and vegetables, had his rooms painted green and furnished with a green sofa, green chairs, a green table, a green bed and green curtains. His gig, his livery, his portmanteau, his gloves and his whip were all green. He wore a green silk handkerchief, and a large watch-chain with green seals was fastened to the green buttons of his green waistcoat. Dressed thus, he promenaded daily on the Steyne, as proud as a peacock and as green as a parrot. He was the talk of the town, turning all his admirers green with envy. Then something terrible happened..."

"Yes," I prompted.

"The worst thing possible. To anyone interested in scaling the heights of fashion it was the most terrible thing imaginable. He was criticised in the newspapers. In 1806 the *Lewes and Brighthelmstone Journal* published a poem about the Green Man of Brighton and, as I happen to know it by heart, I shall recite it to you.

> A spruce little man in a doublet of green
> Perambulates daily the streets and the Steyne.
> Green striped is his waistcoat, his small-clothes are green,
> And oft round his neck a green 'kerchief is seen.

Green watch-string, green seals, and, for certain, I've heard,
(Tho' they're powdered) green whiskers, and eke a green beard.
Green garters, green hose, and, deny it who can,
The brains, too, are green, of this green little man!

"Poor Henry Cope couldn't cope with the criticism. A fortnight later he attempted suicide by throwing himself from the window of his lodging on the South Parade. Finding that he wasn't dead, finding, in fact, that he wasn't even particularly injured, he got up, ran to the nearby cliff and threw himself over the precipice to the beach below. Finding that he still wasn't dead, though badly bruised, he went quite mad and spent the remainder of his days in a straitjacket. And that is the story of the Green Man of Brighton who fell from the heights of fashion and suffered a fate worse than death."

As Yore finished recounting the tale of the Green Man, I remembered the electric blue man who was last seen in the company of Yo!

"Where's Yet?" I asked.

"Wallowing in mud somewhere," Yo! replied. "About an hour or so after you left us, the effects of the magic button began to wear off. As it did so, he sank closer and closer to the ground. Eventually his feet actually touched the earth but, almost immediately, they began to sink beneath it. Then that freaky outfit he was wearing changed back to a claret in colour and he became thoroughly miserable. I left him crying like a baby, up to his neck in mud and telling me he wanted to be alone."

"It gives a whole new meaning to that sinking feeling," I said.

"At the moment it is the sun which is sinking," Yore interjected, "and we want to be in Blackboys before dark. We'd best be going."

"*You'd* best be going," said Yo!, "I think I'll just hang around here for a while."

"Don't you want to try out your new boots?" I said.

"What? And get them muddy? No fear. These boots are not made for walking."

THE THREE YS MEN

"Boots not made for walking," Yore repeated sullenly, shaking his head and setting off towards the setting sun. I bid Yo! a further farewell and followed.

From that moment on, Yore's boots were certainly made for walking because he set a gruelling pace. We had already covered a dozen miles, but he said we had a further six to complete before the day was out. And as the day was nearly out there was no time to lose.

We passed the time and the miles in relative silence, skirting Selwyns Wood and bypassing the village of Roser's Cross which Yore told me was named, according to legend, after an occult sect which practised witchcraft during the fifteenth century. In any event, he informed me, it was now free of all such practices and was a thoroughly pleasant and peaceful village. I never had the opportunity to find out because we pressed onward until, eventually, we reached the village of Blackboys, named after the Black Boy inn. Desperate for an excuse to rest, I suggested we stop at the inn for refreshment. To my surprise, Yore refused. He had to be in Uckfield that evening and he could not tarry. I panicked. I had seen the signs. Uckfield was a further five miles! Reading my mind, Yore smiled and told me he knew a large house in Stonebridge, the next hamlet. Although he would go to Uckfield, I could stay the night there.

Ten minutes later we were outside the house. Yore told me he would see me in the morning, exactly as he had promised the previous night in Robertsbridge. Now, however, I had no intention of seeking to avoid him. I had enjoyed his companionship throughout the day and would willingly accompany him through the rest of his county. I stood at the gate and watched as he strode off in the gathering gloom.

The Twenty-first of April, 1996

The dawn had dawned on me slowly. Although I had slept deeply, or so it seemed, I had been accompanied throughout the night by the most puzzling dreams. But the most puzzling thing of all was waking up and slowly becoming aware that yesterday's reality was more bizarre than last night's dreams. Disconcerting. Disorientating.

Clambering out of bed and shuffling across the room, I pulled the curtains open. Early morning sunlight streamed in, washing away yesterday's mystereality with today's reality. The sun! It was another beautiful day. Two in a row. Unusual for April.

Fifteen minutes later I had gone downstairs for breakfast. Free range eggs from the farm across the road and sausages made to the local butcher's own recipe. These facts, gleaned from the middle-aged lady who was the owner of the house, further cheered me.

As I ate, I thought about yesterday's events. In particular, Yore's promise to see me in the morning. Although the prospect of having a ghostly guide still caused an element of apprehension, my principal feeling was an earnest desire that he should materialise.

Materialise. I smiled. One could not even take everyday words for granted when Yore was around.

The middle-aged lady returned to clear my plates.

"What brings you to these parts?" she asked.

"Oh, I had a few days off so I thought I'd get away for awhile."

"Are you walking?"

"Yes."

"We get a lot of walkers. I suppose you are doing the Wealdway."

"Not exactly."

I was relieved that the inexact nature of my reply hadn't elicited any further questions. Evidently, she was only making polite small-talk and was not particularly interested in what I was doing.

Come to think of it, what was I doing? I liked Yore's idea that we should walk from one end of Sussex to the other but I hadn't a clue where I was going. I hadn't a map. I had relied totally on Yore as a guide. If he didn't turn up this morning I was lost. Literally.

It was with trepidation that I stepped out into the morning air ten minutes later.

Reaching the quiet country lane on which the house stood, I looked apprehensively from left to right, scanning the landscape for some sign of my ghostly guide. Nothing. If he was here in spirit he certainly wasn't here in body.

Oh well. I had to do something. A decision was required. Left or right? I chose left. Strolling aimlessly down the lane, I became aware that I was still haunted by Yore's odd sense of humour. The Ghost of Sussex Past was late! Or perhaps he was early. Yes that was it! Sussex Past. He had been and gone already! Sussex Passed!

"I told you that the Past is always with you."

It was Yore! My heart lifted. I looked round but I couldn't see him.

"And I told you also that the Past is always visible to those who have their eyes open. Open your eyes."

I turned round again and there he was. His rotund yet robust frame squatting on a stile.

"Am I pleased to see you!" I said. "I thought you had deserted me."

"I am not permitted to desert you. I have my orders. And in any case, this particular penance is a pleasure!"

"One question," I asked, "how did you know I would choose left? If I had chosen right, I would have walked in the opposite direction while you were sitting here waiting for me."

He smiled: "If you had chosen right I would have been there and not here, telling you to come here and not there. But in choosing left you chose right. Right was right but now it's wrong. Left is now right."

"Thank you," I said, "for answering my question with such clarity."

He smiled again: "I'm sorry. I couldn't resist. Allow me to explain. I had planned originally to go right this morning. That is, north. My intention was to skirt Uckfield to the north so that we could follow the footsteps I took through my county all those years ago. On my original walk, I had taken the north-west passage via Fletching, Ardingly and Pease Pottage, the diversion being necessary to avoid the Unholy Places."

"The Unholy Places?"

"Yes, even Holy Sussex has her Unholy Places. Her Sodom and Gomorrah."

"Sodom and Gomorrah? In Sussex!"

"Yes indeed, though you probably know them under their worldly names. Haywards Heath and Burgess Hill."

I laughed. "And I suppose that those who look upon Haywards Heath and Burgess Hill turn to pillars of salt!"

"Worse, they turn to gold."

Yore fell silent. Deep in thought. Or prayer. Then he continued.

"Either way I was not prepared to pass through the Unholy Places even in those days. I am sure they are worse now. But the disease has spread and now even the north-west passage is blocked. Pease Pottage is no more. It has been eaten alive by the infernos. Like ants, they swarm over and round it as they pass between their nest in London and the Unholy Places. We cannot go there. No, the only way through lies to the south. Which," he said more cheerfully, "is why left is right. We head south!"

He rose, mounted the stile with deceptive ease, and passed over into the field beyond. I followed. It was not a pretty sight. Not so much a field as a huge prairie. Yore read my thoughts.

"Ugly isn't it? I remember when there were half a dozen separate fields here. The hedges and trees were ripped up as a sacrifice to the godget of gold."

THE THREE YS MEN

We passed over the prairie in silence. Soon we came to the grounds of Pembroke Manor and crossed a fence into them. My spirits lifted. We were welcomed by a beautifully landscaped garden, liberally sprinkled with trees, which led down to two large lakes. The manor house itself, standing resplendant in full sunlight, was a fine example of English architecture.

Having passed through the entire length of the grounds, we crossed a lane and followed the northern banks of a stream. This we crossed beside another fine old English house. Thence via a track which passed through the village of Palehouse Common we came to Crockstead Farm, a large equestrian centre.

"Dressage," Yore remarked simply, gesturing in the direction of a horse and rider.

We decided to rest awhile and watch.

Minutes passed as we sat in silent appreciation of the subtle unity of man and beast. Then I caught something bright and blue in the corner of my eye. I looked up and gasped. Floating down towards us was the fat, cherubic figure of Yet and, on his shoulders, Yo!, dressed as a cowboy and waving a sombrero frantically.

"Yeeehaaar!!"

I expected the sight and sound of the ghostriders in the sky to cause the horses to stampede. But they carried on, unspooked by the spooks. Clearly, neither Yet nor Yo! could be seen or heard by those around us. This puzzled me. I knew that Yet was invisible but Yore had told me yesterday that Yo! could be seen by anyone.

"He can be seen by anyone, but not at anytime," Yore explained. "He is not allowed to make an exhibition of himself. What would *He* say if the antics of Yo! found its way into the newspapers and the whole of Sussex became full of ghosthunters and reporters. No, He would not like it so He doesn't allow it. Simple."

"You mean that discretion is the greater part of Valhalla," said Yo!, dismounting from Yet.

"Yards!" said Yet.
"Valhalla has nothing to do with it," said Yore, ignoring the second comment.
"Oh, I don't know," said Yo! "that was quite a Wagnerian entrance, don't you think? The ride of the Valkyries!"
I laughed. Looking up at the bobbing blob above me, I could see Yo!'s point. Yet looked like a cross between an overweight Wagnerian tenor and an extremely camp Brunnhilde. And that's the shape of things to come, I thought, sniggering.
"God help us!" Yore replied, grinning grimly.
"Yards!" said Yet.
"Is that all you can say?" said Yore, looking up at the blob.
"Yards!" said the blob.
"Am I right in assuming that you have a somewhat limited vocabulary?" Yore remarked, repeating himself with more vocabulary.
"And what does it mean?" I asked.
"Yards? Yards is yards!" Yet replied.
"Well done!" I said mockingly, "you managed to string four words together."
"Incorrect," Yore responded, "he managed to string two words together."
"It's mega-simple-powerplay. Yards is yards and avant-garde is avant-garde and never the twain shall meet."
"Yes," I repeated patiently, "but what is the definition of yards. What does it mean?"
"Mean? Its meaning? That's a good question. I've never thought about it before."
"Yo!" said Yo!, "that's a good answer. Wicked!"
"It may or may not be a wicked answer," replied Yore, "but it is certainly not a good one."
"Well," Yet continued thoughtfully, "the definition of yards is that which isn't avant-garde. And the definition of avant-garde is that which isn't yards. Is that yards?"

"Yards!" exclaimed Yo!
"Avant-garde!" I protested.
"Oh my God!" moaned Yore. "I think it must be time to go."
"Indeed it must," agreed Yo!, "you take the low road and we'll take the high road, and we'll be on the Downs before you! Yet! Let's get high!"
"Get high? Mega-yards-powerplay!"
In an instant, Yo! had grabbed Yet by the ankle and they took off at speed, heading south-west.
After the blob had become a dot in the distance and disappeared, my thoughts returned to earth. It was then that I became aware of a strange paradox. Gazing at the utopian serenity of the dressage event taking place before me, and comparing it with the surreal scene I had just witnessed, it almost seemed that the equestrianism was unreal. The contrast was too large to be conceived. Perspective was impossible. Which was real?
"This is real," Yore replied simply. "Let's go."
Leaving Crockstead Farm behind us, we followed a footpath south-west which turned right after half a mile and led up to a quiet country lane. This we followed for a mile and a half before taking a footpath across a field into woodland which bordered Plashett Park, another private estate with beautifually landscaped gardens. Emerging from the woods and crossing a road, we followed a stream until we arrived at the village of Isfield.
"Ah!" exclaimed Yore as we arrived at the village. "We shall rest here awhile. This village has a wonderful inn, the Laughing Fish."
I followed Yore into the inn.
"You shall have to pay," he said simply as we reached the bar. "No money. Not since I died. Not allowed in Sufferance. Not needed."
Relieved that the woman behind the bar had not heard what he said, I ordered two pints of Beard's Best. We then went outside where the sound of birdsong greeted us. I took

a long draught of the ale. My eyes closed in pleasure as the flavours caressed my palate. Smokey with a strong hoppy aftertaste.

"Beards," said Yore. "Good isn't it?"

"Very good!" I exclaimed enthusiastically.

Yore continued: "Beards is a Lewes brewery. Or at least it was. It's in Hailsham now. But Harveys brewery is still in Lewes and the brewery building still dominates the town centre there. As indeed is only fitting for a fine old Sussex town. Only a church or a brewery should have pride of place in a town. And every good town should have both!"

He took another healthy gulp of his ale, licked the foam from his lips and continued.

"Let me tell you about Harveys brewery. It is a good example of sound economics. All the raw materials come from the land and all the by-products return to it. The malt dust and small and broken barley corns are fed to chickens and the residues from the wort are fed to dairy cattle. Did you know, for instance, that spent grains in the brewing process contribute to an estimated 27 pints of milk for every barrel of beer brewed?"

"No, I didn't," I said, smiling. In truth, I didn't even know what wort was, let alone the alleged benefits of feeding its residues to cows.

"And did you know that the spent hops in the brewing process are used as organic compost? And that the surplus yeast is fed to pigs?"

"No!" I laughed. "But I'm suitably impressed. Very eco-friendly."

Yore frowned: "I don't know the current jargon. But it's good economics."

"Yes," I said.

Yore took another quaff of ale, and nodded sagely.

"Very good ale. No doubt about it. But do you know what I really desire now? A pint of the barley brew from the brewery closest my heart. Closest my heart because closest my hearth. It was the brewery nearest my home during my worldly life. Michell's of Horsham."

"Michells of Horsham? I can't say I've ever heard of it."

"No, and you won't," Yore replied sadly. "Michell's ale is no more. Extinct. Gone forever. The brewery was taken over by the Rock Brewery in 1911 and then by Whitbread. Alas, I shall never again taste Michell's ale."

He sipped at his beer in silence for a while before his countenance brightened again.

"Mind you," he said, "Horsham still boasts a fine brewery. King and Barnes! Ah, their Festive Ale! And their new Broadwood Bitter! Bliss! Well almost, as near as this world gets anyway."

"Well," I interjected, placing my newly emptied glass on the table, "you will have to make do with another pint of Beard's Best."

He seemed happy enough with the compromise so I replenished our glasses and returned to my seat in the garden. As soon as I had done so, Yore resumed his monologue:

"Now that you know all about Sussex breweries I shall tell you about Sussex inns. Take this inn for instance. Many times I've got someone to stand me the price of a pint in this inn."

"I see that things haven't changed much in that regard!"

"Yes, but it was more difficult when I was alive in the worldly sense. I had money then. It's not easy getting someone to stand the price of a pint when one has money in one's pocket. Then it becomes a question of stealth. The easiest way was by challenging a stranger to a game of ringing-the-bull."

"Ringing-the-bull?"

"Yes, a good Sussex inn game. It was very popular in this particular pub. The rules were simple. A player sat with his back to the wall underneath a huge bull's head with a hook on its nose. From the ceiling hung a length of cord with a ring on the end. The object was to get the ring up and onto the hook on the bull's nose. The ring was given a kind of jerk, so that it swung backwards and upwards onto the hook. The loser paid for the drinks."

Yore paused for breath and for another sip of ale.

"But in the Blackboys Inn which we passed yesterday they used to play ringing-the-stag. Instead of a bull's head, there was a stag's head on the wall with a hook on its nose. The rules were different too. The player stood in front of the stag's head, not under it, and several feet away. The object was the same, namely to get the ring onto the hook, but because of the positioning of the player the trick was to swing the ring in a curve. And as the ring was filled with lead and weighed about a pound it was not advisable to stand in the way of play!"

As Yore concluded his eulogy on Sussex ales and inns he fell silent, staring wistfully into his glass. The conversation had dried up and so, within a minute or so, had the beer. Staring wistfully at my own empty glass, I realised, with regret, that it was time to go.

We followed the road south from Isfield for several hundred yards before taking a footpath, heading west, which runs parallel to a dismantled railway line. Crossing fields and then a stream, we approached the Anchor Inn which stood invitingly in a peaceful and isolated location on the banks of the River Ouse. Ignoring the invitation we pressed onwards over tracks, fields and small roads until we had crossed Bevern Stream and, in so doing, had bypassed Barcombe Cross to the north. Striding westward relentlessly, I admired the Downs, resplendant in all their majesty, looming ever closer. Soon they were scarcely two miles to the south.

"They have come north to meet us," said Yore. "Tomorrow morning we shall feel their embrace."

"Tell me," I said, "isn't there a huge figure carved into the side of the Downs somewhere? I'm sure I once read something about it, but I can't quite remember what it was."

"There are several figures carved into the Downs. There is a magnificent white horse carved into the side of a hill in the vale of Cuckmere. It's as good as any in the country. But I suspect you are referring to the Long Man of Wilmington."

"Yes, I think that's it," I concurred excitedly. "Will we see it?"

"It does not lie on the route of our pilgrimage but is half a day's walk to the south-east."

He pointed to the left behind us to signify the direction.

"That's a pity. I bet it's well worth seeing."

"Indeed it is. It is Europe's largest representation of the human form."

"But how did it get there in the first place?"

"That's a good question. One that continues to baffle modern scholars. Some say it's prehistoric. Others point to fourth century Roman coins bearing a similar figure, or Anglo-Saxon ornaments with a helmeted figure looking remarkably like the Long Man. Still others claim that it was the work of an artistic monk from the neighbouring Priory. It may even be another wonderful folly."

"Not Squire Fuller surely?"

"No," Yore grinned. "I'm afraid Honest Jack can't claim the credit for this one! It's certainly been on the slopes of Windover Hill since the start of the eighteenth century, a hundred years before Squire Fuller's dramatic arrival on the scene."

"So what you are really saying is that nobody knows."

"No, that is not what I am saying at all. I am saying that it baffles modern scholars. Prehistoric, Roman, Anglo-Saxon, Medieval, Modern. They haven't a clue. Or, rather, they have clues but not enough of them to lead them to the answer. But the fact that it continues to fool the scientists does not mean that nobody knows the Long Man's secret."

"Who does then?"

"I do."
"And what is it?"
"I am not at liberty to say."
"Why not?"
"Because it is a secret."

I felt exasperated but realised that further questioning would be futile. If Yore knew the secret he was going to keep it and there was nothing I could do to prize it from him. I remained in exactly the same predicament as the scientists. Baffled.

Yore smiled reassuringly: "I shall, however, tell you the Legend of the Long Man of Wilmington. It was told to me by an old shepherd who tended his flock near Alfriston in the early years of this century. Besides, the Legend of the Long Man is far more interesting than his Secret."

"Go on," I mumbled, unconvinced and still feeling cheated.

"Once upon a time there were two giants," he began. "They were both Sussex giants because one lived on Mount Caburn and the other lived on Windover Hill. This, of course, made them neighbours because the two peaks are only four miles apart which, for giants, is no distance at all - a couple of dozen strides to be precise. Of course, if they had been giants from Kent it would have been more like a hundred strides, the Kentish variety being far smaller and much more feeble. But I digress. The other thing to be remembered is that they lived in happier times than now. In those times, everybody had plenty of work and, more to the point, everybody enjoyed their work. They worked everyday except for Holy Days, Saints Days, solstices, equinoxes and other Feast Days. There were no Bank Holidays because there were no banks, but, strangely enough, nobody seemed to mind. But I digress again. Anyway, the two giants worked as flint-crackers. Everyday except for Holy Days, Saints Days, solstices, equinoxes and other Feast Days they worked on the side of their respective hills cracking flints with enormous hammers the size of oak trees. Each giant did the work of fifty men but nobody minded. The men had plenty of other work to do on the land and the broken flints provided the stone with which the people built the cottages they lived in. Everybody was very happy."

"So what went wrong?" I asked pre-emptively.

"Ah, there lies the moral of the tale. They forgot the second great Commandment of Christ."

"The Second Commandment?" My mind struggled desperately for a fragmentary memory of my woefully inadequate religious education. "You mean they took the name of God in vain!" I said triumphantly.

"Only inasmuch as they forgot the second great Commandment of Christ."

"Pardon?" I said, perplexed.

"The second great Commandment: To love thy neighbour as thyself."

"Oh!" I said, still puzzled. "I thought you were talking of the Ten Commandments."

"No, only the Two. You are confusing the Ten Commandments given to Moses with the Two Commandments given by Christ."

"Oh," I replied. "We were obviously speaking at cross purposes."

"Very good!"

"Pardon?"

"Very good! The pun on Cross purposes. One of the best I've heard for ages."

The pun was neither intended, nor comprehended, but I let it stand. The conversation had become obscure enough already without the creation of another tangent for Yore to travel down.

"Shall I continue with the story?" he continued, still chuckling at the unintended pun.

"You've started," I said indifferently, "so you may as well finish."

"Well, as I was saying, the two giants, being

neighbours, forgetting the commandment to love each other, began to quarrel. The whole of Sussex could hear them as they bellowed abuse at each other across the four mile gap between them. Suddenly, the Mount Caburn giant, in a rage, hurled his hammer with all his might at his rival on Windover Hill. He scored a direct hit, striking him between the eyes and the Windover Hill giant fell dead to the ground. Now, being a Sussex giant and not one of the smaller Kentish variety, he was far too heavy to move so they buried him where he lay. And that's his outline you can see to this day, in the exact place where he lies happily ever after."

"Thanks for the fairy story," I said, relieved that it was over.

"It was not a fairy story. How can a story about giants be a fairy story? But if you'd like a fairy story, I could tell you plenty of stories about Sussex fairies. They live under the ground."

I was resigned to enduring another Sussex folk-tale, but at that very moment Yore was interrupted by a deep rumbling noise from under the ground. Images of Sussex fairies danced in my head. More alarmingly, the sudden prospect of a long-dead giant becoming exhumed and resurrected in the field in which we stood filled me with dismay - not least, because it was bound to be a Sussex giant and not a feeble Kentish specimen.

I stared earnestly at Yore for some sign of reassurance but he looked as mysified as I. Glurghh! With a squelch of liberation a human skull surfaced from the mud. Eyelessly it grinned at us but said nothing. Not surprising really. Who ever heard of a skeleton speaking?

"Ouch! Magpie! Get your hands off me! Megamag!! Ow! Don't do that! Double-plus-ungood! Put that thing away! Mega-avant-garde-powerplay!"

In a second the familiar face of Yet surfaced, dislodging the skull and a host of other human bones as he did so. He was clearly in considerable distress.

"Ow! Oooh! Leave me alone! Ouch! Megamag! Mind where you're putting that thing! Don't you dare! Yeeaarrgh!!"

Pressing the magic button in desperation, he took off like a rocket, scattering skeletal remains all over the field as he did so. We watched in amazement as he shot away, muttering mega-expletives and rubbing his painful posterior. His trajectory took him over Mount Harry and out of sight.

Looking back at that part of the field which had served as his launch-pad, it looked as though a bomb had exploded. Fibulas, tibias and dozens of other human bones protruded above the surface. And there, standing erect, in the exact spot where Yet had been only moments earlier, was an enormous broadsword. It looked very sharp, if a little rusty, and I suddenly realised the cause of poor Yet's distress. Ouch! I thought, sympathising with both his plight and his imminent need for flight.

Then the strangest thing happened. The sword, in an impressive imitation of Excalibur, sank slowly beneath the soil of Sussex. Moments later the same soil seemed to liquify so that the bones sank out of sight also. Finally, the field appeared exactly as it had done a minute or so prior to the disturbance.

"*Requiescant in pace*," Yore stated solemnly, crossing himself and bowing his head for a moment.

"Was this field some kind of graveyard?" I asked.

"I suppose you could say it was a graveyard of sorts. It was a battlefield. Upon this spot and all over the surrounding countryside from Lewes to Plumpton thousands of people perished in one of the bloodiest battles in human history."

"Which battle was that?"

"It is known to posterity as the Battle of Lewes."

"I've never heard of it."

"Then you show the Present's lack of respect for the Past."

"Probably," I responded, feeling genuinely contrite.

"And Yet showed the Future's lack of respect for the Past by disturbing the souls of the slain. And, as we have witnessed, he paid dearly for it."

"He paid painfully for it!" I said, wincing at the memory of the up-pointed sword.

Yore grinned: "The Future ignores the Past at its own peril."

We climbed over a stile and ascended the hill to East Chiltington. Seated on the grass verge opposite the church, we bathed in the peacefulness of our surroundings. Only the birds disturbed the silence. East Chiltington, I decided, was my favourite of all the villages we had discovered so far.

After a few minutes we rose and continued our journey. As we sallied forth, Yore endeavoured to teach me about the Battle of Lewes. I learned that it had taken place in 1264 between the armies of King Henry the Third and those of the barons under the command of Simon de Montfort. But after a while my attention started to wander as Yore, who was obviously an expert on the subject, discussed each side's respective strategies. Realising that my thoughts were elsewhere, and no doubt feeling exasperated at my wilful ignorance of the past, he fell into silence.

We walked on, ever-westward, watching the sun sink lower before us and admiring the ever-present Downs to our left. After a couple of miles the village of Streat greeted us with a fine old house and a fine old church. Resisting the temptation to take a further rest, in spite of our growing weariness, we strode onwards. It was then that a further thought crossed my mind. I was certainly weary, having walked the whole day through, but was Yore? Did the Ghost of Sussex Past feel tired?

"Of course," he replied, not waiting to be asked. "Feeling tired is part of the pleasure of exertion. Where would be the pleasure of drinking beer, if one couldn't taste the bitterness of the hops? And where would be the pleasure of walking all day, if one couldn't taste the pleasure of a well-earned rest at the end of it? No, I don't *need* to feel weary but I choose to. One must have the pain in order to have the pleasure."

I felt sure that Yo! would have disagreed heartily with Yore's logic and I wished that he were here to argue his case. For my part, I was not certain that I fully understood his reasoning. Indeed, to someone brought up with the teaching of Freud there seemed something almost unhealthy about Yore's masochistic philosophy.

"Freud is a fraud," Yore remarked simply.

As my companion was replying to my thoughts, we turned a corner and were confronted by a powerful smell and an unpleasant sight. I knew the smell. Pigs. And I knew the sight. A factory farm. I felt sickened. Then it occurred to me that I had been given a heaven-sent opportunity to make a case against Yore's earlier statement.

"If you say that pain and suffering are so good," I began, "how can you justify this?"

"I can't justify this. It is unjustifiable. There is all the difference in the world between choosing to endure pain voluntarily for some greater good and inflicting pain cruelly on creatures who do not choose it."

"That's all very well and very high-sounding," a voice replied, "but how do you propose to feed the huge populations in our cities without places like this? They may not be nice but they are necessary."

The words were not mine, not least because I didn't agree with them. They were Yo!'s. He stood waiting for us as we turned the corner of the track beside the factory farm. On his head was the American baseball cap, back-to-front. As if to be deliberately provocative, he was munching greedily on a fast-food hamburger.

He spoke with his mouth full and thrust the burger towards me: "Want some?"

"No thanks," I replied. "I don't."

"You don't eat meat?" he asked.
"I eat meat. I don't eat burgers."
"Weird," he responded, dismissively.
I was angry: "And I don't agree with what you just said about places like this."
"In that case," he said nonchalently, "how do you propose to feed the populations in our cities?"
"I don't know," I admitted, "but a gut feeling tells me that, in cases like this, the end doesn't justify the means."
"In cases like this," he countered, "if the end doesn't justify the means it means starvation in the end!"
"Witty but witless," said Yore, joining in the fray. "There is no need for starvation, merely a need for sacrifice. It all comes back to my original point. People must endure minor pains and inconveniences in order to choose the higher good. If people refrained from eating cruelly produced meat and only ate free-range food, the suffering of farm animals in the future would be lessened and places like this would cease to exist."
"Idealistic rubbish!" exclaimed Yo!. "You are kicking against human nature. People will always choose convenience before inconvenience. Selfishness before selflessness. Comfort before sacrifice."
"Perhaps," Yore replied sadly, "but comfort is the great corrupter and the self is one's own worst enemy."
"There is only one path that humanity will ever take," Yo! continued, "and that's the path of least resistance."
"That path leads straight to Hell," said Yore solemnly.
"It leads straight to Hell on earth for these pigs!" I asserted.
"The issue is clear," Yore continued, "either people pay a little extra for free-range meat or they will get what they deserve."
"Yep!" said Yo!, "they will get exactly what they deserve. Cheap pork!"
With this final triumphant exclamation, he wiped the remains of the relish from his chin and threw the

polystyrene container into the field. To my disgust I watched as a slight gust of wind cartwheeled the carton away from us. When I looked up, Yo! had gone.

Yore said nothing. Strolling purposefully into the field, he retrieved the carton, placed it in his pocket and returned.

"Pigs," he said, smiling broadly, "let's talk about pigs. Better still, let's talk about Sussex pigs."

We set off once more towards the setting sun, never getting any closer to it but content in the knowledge that we had almost reached Ditchling, the day's destination, where we would rest for the night. It was less than two miles away, enough time for Yore to enthuse about the Sacred Sussex Pig.

"Pigs have always been sacred to the people of my county," he began. "Not sacred in any idolatrous sense, you understand. The sacred pig was never like the Sacred Cow. Heaven forbid! Let's just say that the humble pig has always held a special place in the hearts of the people of Sussex, which is why that place we have just passed is so utterly un-Sussex. In fact, it's been said that the crest of Sussex should be a pig sitting on its haunches, and underneath should be the motto, 'You may push and you may shuv but I tell'ee I won't be druv.'

"I will tell you," he continued, warming to his subject and pointing to the high Downs to our left, "our love affair with the pig is as old as those hills. In the days when the great forest of Andrieda stretched across the whole of the county for about sixty miles from east to west, shrouding Sussex in mystery, the ancient Celts valued the pork which the forest could sustain above all other meats.

"Later, when the Saxons came to these shores and gave the county its name of Sussex - South Saxons - they valued the pig, or boar, for more than simply its meat. They believed that an effigy of a little bronze boar worn on their armour would protect them in time of battle. But they valued its meat also and it was always the principal dish at their great Yule feast when they celebrated the Winter Solstice. On the night of Yule, or so they believed, Freya, the goddess of fertility and fruitfulness, rode across the sky in a chariot drawn by a boar with a golden hide, scattering the seeds of everything that grew, and so ensuring a fruitful year to come. Later, when the true God was accepted by the South Saxons and the old gods driven out, the love affair with the pig continued.

"When the Normans arrived, defeating the Saxons on Sussex soil near Hastings, nothing changed as far as the pig was concerned. The Normans, like the Saxons before them, considered pork the most fitting dish for a feast. But now the Pagan feast of Yule had been replaced by the birthday Mass of Christ and the Normans considered a boar's head an essential part of their Christmas celebrations. It was brought into the halls of their kings on a golden dish to the accompaniment of instruments and the singing of hymns. Old religions had died, old kingdoms had passed away, but the sacred Sussex pig remained!"

"It's all a far cry from the suffering of those poor creatures back there," I said when he had finished. "That farm was truly barbaric."

"It was neither truly a farm nor truly barbaric. It deserves neither compliment. A true farm lives in harmony with the natural surroundings upon which it relies. What we saw back there was nothing but an industrial factory for producing meat. Neither was it barbarian because barbarians were close enough to the natural scheme of things to fatten their own pigs and, yes, to slaughter their own pigs when the time came. What we saw back there was a monument to a gutless age that wants the convenience of pre-packaged meat without the responsibilities that go with it. This generation wants its cake but doesn't know how to bake it, and wants its meat but doesn't know how to treat it."

"So all is lost," I muttered sombrely.

"Perhaps, perhaps not. I am not gifted with the ability

to see the future. But if I can't know the future I can at least hope in it. There is hope, I am sure."

"I wish I had your faith."

"I was not speaking of faith, but of hope. They are quite distinct. I have hope in the future, I have precious little faith in it. I put my faith in more reliable things."

"Okay," I said resignedly, "I wish I had your hope then. The future looks pretty hopeless as far as I can see."

"Well, in that case," Yore replied, smiling reassuringly and placing his hand on my shoulder, "let's thank God that you can't see very far!"

I smiled. Paradoxically, the weight of Yore's hand on my shoulders had taken a weight from them. I felt happier and Yore, sensing my change of mood, continued more cheerfully.

"Any way," he resumed, "you interrupted my hymn of praise to the sacred Sussex pig. I shall now bring the story up to date. Well, up to date for me. Not quite up to date for you. But I ask you to allow an old man to wallow in nostalgia for a few moments."

"Be my guest," I said, smiling.

"When I was a young boy living in a village near Arundel during the late 1870's, I remember that nearly every Sussex villager kept a pig in the sty in the back garden. The pigs were turned out every morning to wander away to find a nice spot where they could lie all day. It was a common sight in the morning to see the pigs ambling through the village searching for that special spot. Then, in the early evening, one would see them ambling home again when it was feeding time."

"Now that's what I call free-range!" I laughed.

"You have to understand that keeping pigs in those days was all a question of good economics. Each pig was a solid investment. And, believe me, investments don't come much more solid than a fully fattened pig! When it was killed it supplied meat for a very long time. Every part of it was eaten, from the tips of its ears to the tips of its trotters."

"Urghh! I'm not sure I like the sound of pig's trotters!"

"Oh, but you haven't tried them," Yore protested. "A cold boiled trotter was considered a very satisfying snack. When I was a little older and began to frequent the inns of my county, one would often see the 'trotter man' doing his rounds. He would wander through the town, from inn to inn, calling 'Trotters! hot trotters!', carrying the trotters in a large wooden tray on his head."

"I'm still not convinced, I'm afraid!"

"The loss is yours entirely. But I digress. I believe I was about to explain the intricacies of pig economics. The other advantage was that the fatted pig, once killed, brought the community closer together. You see, in the days before the arrival of the godgets, it was not easy to eat the whole of one's own pig before the meat went off. Of course, one could always cure one's pig in order to preserve it, something I was rather expert at during my worldly life, but that is another matter. But on the assumption that one didn't wish to cure one's own pig, it was common practice to distribute the pork joints to one's neighbours. This was an excellent and highly efficient way of storing food because the neighbours would eat the joints and then, when they, in turn, killed their own pigs, the gifts of pork would be returned."

"Well," I said, grinning broadly, "at least I am no longer pig ignorant."

"Very good!" Yore replied, reflecting my grin with a broad one of his own. "But that raises another topic of conversation."

"Really?" I said, surprised that a casual witticism could be a cause for further dialogue or, since Yore was doing all the talking, for further monologue.

"Yes," Yore resumed, "the English language. Pigs don't speak it, of course, but they have contributed richly towards it."

"Go on," I prompted, intrigued.

"Well, to give you but one example, do you know

where the phrase 'to let the cat out of the bag' comes from?"

"No I don't, now I come to think about it, but it's a phrase I know and use sometimes. It means to give the game away."

"Precisely, but did you know that the game which was given away by the cat involved a pig?"

"No," I answered, confused.

"In days of old, if a man wished to sell a piglet, he would take it to market in a small sack called a poke, which, incidentally, is where the word pocket comes from, a small poke. But, as I was saying, he would take his piglet to market in a poke and a purchaser would often buy it without looking inside, the presence of the pig being felt readily through the poke. And this is where the phrase 'to buy a pig in a poke' comes from, a term still used to describe a deal in which the purchaser has to take a great deal on trust. It was said, however, that certain dishonest traders would sometimes deceive a simpleton by selling him a cat instead of a pig. But cats, being cats, and not wishing to be kept in a poke, would often escape before the transaction could be completed. In this case, the dishonest trader would have 'let the cat out of the bag' and the game would be up!"

As Yore concluded his aphoristic tale, we found ourselves walking through the quiet witterns on the outskirts of Ditchling. Eventually we emerged on the road which runs through the centre of the village. Looking to my right I spied an inn sign. The Bull. My heart lifted. I felt tired, hungry and thirsty and the inn provided the ideal remedy for all three complaints. It seemed that Yore had exactly the same idea.

"The Bull!" he exclaimed, with obvious satisfaction. "That reminds me of another well-known saying with roots in antiquity. The South Saxons, in their drinking matches, used to drink from large double-handled tankards, fitted with pegs inside. If one drinker uncovered more pegs in one draught than his opponent he would say in triumph

THE THREE YS MEN

'Ah! I've taken you down a peg!'"

"That sounds good," I replied, relishing the prospect of the first taste of ale on my lips, "tonight I'm going to take you down a peg or two!"

My first impressions of the Bull, gleaned as we crossed the threshold, were entirely favourable. Old oak beams spanned the ceiling and a large open fireplace stacked with logs held out the promise of a warm welcome to travellers such as ourselves.

"The inn is Elizabethan, it dates back to 1569," said Yore, confirming with his words what my eyes had already guessed.

The first priority was to obtain two pints of ale and, not needing to be told whose round it was, I went to the bar while Yore found a table in the corner. I returned with two pints of bitter.

"Hmmm," muttered Yore after taking the first sip, "I'm not sure I recognise this one. What is it?"

"Brakspeare's," I answered, "apparently it's from Henley-on-Thames."

"It's not from Sussex?"

He took a longer draught of ale, paused for the aftertaste and smiled. "No matter, it is good English ale none the less! Henley-on-Thames, you say. Hmmm. Oxfordshire. If an ale is not fortunate enough to come from Sussex, there are no better places from which it may come than Oxfordshire!"

I gulped the ale greedily myself, pleased that it met with my companion's approval, and agreeing with his opinion that it was good English ale.

Suddenly there was a monosyllabic breach of the peace.

"Yo!"

Yo!. Oh no! I thought.

"Quite," said Yore.

"May I join you?" he said chirpily, slurping at a can of alcoholic lemonade.

THE THREE YS MEN

"If you must," said Yore with forced patience.

"Oh, come on!" said Yo! plaintively, "what have I done now?"

"Do you need to ask?" I said, still smarting at his *faux pas* at the pig farm.

"Look," he pleaded, "I'm sorry about the way I acted earlier. I was niggled by the naffness of your views. You're so out of touch! You deal with ideal worlds which don't exist, I deal with the real world which does."

Yore responded: "I deal with the ideal because the ideal gives us something to measure reality with. It provides an absolute by which we can judge things objectively."

Yo! was exasperated: "But the ideal doesn't exist so how can you measure things by it!"

"On the contrary," Yore replied, "the ideal always exists, it is merely that we fail to realise it."

"Yore, you're talking trash. Your ideal world may have existed in the past. I don't know and I don't care. Whether it ever existed or whether it's just a figment of your senile imagination, I can't say. But whether it existed or not, once upon a time, it is dead now. Stone dead. As dead as the stone age."

Ignoring Yo!'s latest tirade, Yore continued: "Of course, I mean 'realise' in both senses of the word. Those who realise the existence of the ideal have more chance of realising it. Unfortunately, of course, those who fail to realise the existence of the ideal have no chance of realising it."

I was baffled by the logic and Yo! appeared baffled by what he perceived as the lack of it. There was an awkward silence which was broken eventually by Yo!

"Yo!" he said.

"Yo," I repeated half-heartedly.

"Listen," Yo! continued, "I am really sorry about the way I over-reacted earlier. Whether I was right or wrong I had no right to act that way. I apologise."

"Don't worry about it," I said.

"Buddies?" he asked, thrusting his hand in my direction.

"Buddies," I affirmed, shaking his hand and smiling.

"Buddies?" he asked again, repeating the same procedure with Yore.

"I don't speak American, but if I am correct in the assumption that you wish to affirm friendship I am happy to reciprocate."

Yore took Yo!'s hand, shook it formally, then continued: "The point is my dear Present that you and I are more than friends. We are married. The Past is always wedded to the Present, even when it wishes it wasn't. It is always a marriage, even when it is a marriage of inconvenience."

"In that case," Yo! quipped mischievously, "I want a divorce."

"That which God hath joined together let no man put asunder."

"Why not?"

"Because it is impossible. Our marriage is insoluble in both senses of the word. It is a problem which can neither be solved nor dissolved."

"For God's sake," I exclaimed in exasperation, "this is all getting far too esoteric. Can't we change the subject?"

"Yo!" said Yo!

"Yes," said Yore, "what would you like to talk about?"

"Oh, I don't know. Anything. Anything which is down to earth."

"And not pie in the sky!" exclaimed Yo!

"Or pennies from Heaven," countered Yore.

"Yes," I said, raising my own eyes to Heaven. "Anything easy to understand!"

"In that case," said Yore, "we shall be logical about things."

"Must we?" I complained.

"Yo!" said Yo!

"Yes we must," insisted Yore, "and the logical thing to talk about would be the thing we were talking about before Yo! distracted us."

"Which was?" asked Yo!

"Which was Oxfordshire," replied Yore, "or Henley-on-Thames to be precise. I knew Henley very well during my worldly life. I walked there twice, once from Oxford and once from London."

"I can't say I've ever been there," I said, relieved at the change of subject.

"I think I drove through it once," said Yo!

"Then since neither of you have ever been there I shall tell you about it. I'm sure He won't mind if I allow myself the indulgence of one flight of fancy beyond the borders of my own county. Henley owes its importance, of course, to the main road which runs through it."

"You mean the A4155," said Yo!

"I mean the Thames," said Yore.

"But that's a river!" Yo! protested.

"It was the main highway through England from east to west for hundreds of years, and it was the existence of that highway which breathed life into Henley. During the Middle Ages, it formed the next convenient stopping point down the river from the large Cluniac Abbey at Reading. And it has royal connections also."

"Big deal," muttered Yo!.

Yore, ignoring the interruption, continued. "King Edward the First regularly stayed there whenever he travelled up the Thames from Windsor. And as for the city of Oxford itself, which lies further up that glorious river, it is my favourite place in the whole of England, outside of Sussex. I lived there, studied there and taught there. I think, even now, that a part of me still lives there."

"This menu is naff! No burgers!" exclaimed Yo!, who had obviously become bored with Yore's discourse on the Thames valley.

The mention of food served as a timely reminder that I had still not eaten and, since my glass was also in need of replenishment, I resolved to return to the bar and order both food and drink.

"What would you like to eat?" I asked my two fellow travellers.

Yore pored over the menu for a few moments before looking up resolutely: "I should like the Camembert wedges in cranberry sauce as an *hors d'oeuvre* and the gamekeeper's casserole as a main course. I shall decide upon cheese and dessert later. Oh, and another pint of the Oxfordshire ale."

"Remind me to introduce you to my bank manager," I groaned, grinning grimly.

"Oh, I'd rather not meet one of *those*," Yore remarked anxiously. "I avoided them like the plague during my worldly life. I no longer need to avoid the plague, but I'd rather continue avoiding bank managers if it's all the same to you. It's such a lowly, disreputable profession."

I shook my head in disbelief and turned my attention to Yo!.

"Yo!?" I asked.

"No I don't think so," said Yo! "I need some real food. There must be somewhere in this dead end place where I can get a burger and fries. And any way," he continued, rising to his feet, "I need some action. This pub is the pits. I need sounds! Games! Flashing lights! A pool table! Hip-hop! House! Rave! Acid! TV! Noise! Action!"

With that he sprang into action, leapt over the adjacent table, and strode out of the pub. Yore looked at me and smiled. I shrugged my shoulders and laughed.

"Oh well," I said, "it looks like there's only two for dinner."

Having ordered the food, I returned to the table with two more pints of ale. Yore supped his, smacked his lips in a gesture of satisfaction, and nodded.

"Brakspeare's," he mumbled, mainly to himself. "Yes.

A very good name. Perfectly apt. It is both English and is good enough for the Pope."

"Pardon?"

"I was merely remarking that Brakspeare's is a very good name for an English ale."

"Why?"

"Simply because Brakspeare is a good, traditional English name."

"Because it rhymes with Shakespeare?" I asked, smiling.

"No because it is named after the Pope."

"The Pope."

"Well, not *the* Pope, *a* Pope."

"Pope Brakspeare! Surely not?"

"No, Pope Adrian the Fourth."

"Sorry?"

"Pope Adrian the Fourth."

"Brakspeare's is named after Pope Adrian the Fourth?"

"No, Pope Adrian the Fourth was named after Breakspear."

"I'm afraid you've completely lost me."

"Sorry, am I not making myself clear?"

"Hardly."

"It's simple really. Breakspear became Pope Adrian the Fourth. Nicolas Breakspear. He is the only Englishman ever to be Pope."

"Oh I see!"

"Yes, and that's why I thought Brakspeare's a singularly appropriate name for an English ale. Very English and good enough for the Pope!"

"Right," I said, relieved that the obscure conversation had reached a conclusion.

In fact, the conclusion was timed perfectly because, as we fell temporarily silent, our food arrived.

"We must have wine!" demanded Yore as his Camembert was placed in front of him.

"But you were just singing the praises of the ale," I protested.

"Yes, it is good English ale but this is good French cuisine. It demands wine! It screams out for wine!"

"Okay," I conceded, my heart sinking at this further blow to the health of my wallet. "Red or white."

"Oh, it must be red."

I called over to the man serving behind the bar: "Excuse me, could we please have a bottle of your house red?"

"No! No! No! It must be Burgundy. Only Burgundy will do for a meal like this."

I sighed and shouted over again to the bar: "Sorry, make that a bottle of Burgundy please."

An hour later, we sat sated by the meal and mellowed by the wine we had consumed. A second bottle of Burgundy had been ordered along with a selection of cheeses. I no longer worried about my wallet. It had become numb with the pain and I had become numb with the pleasure. Yore's expression was one of utter contentment. His face aglow, reflecting the colour of the wine.

"I shall sing you a song!" He announced triumphantly.

Almost instantly he seemed to change his mind.

"No, I shan't sing you a song. I am merry. Thank God! But England is not merry. Not any longer. And people are not permitted to sing in inns. If they do they are liable to be arrested or thrown out on the street. And we can't have that. No, certainly not. You are staying in this inn tonight so it wouldn't do to be thrown out on the street, would it?"

"No, it wouldn't." I agreed.

"But," he announced, with renewed resolve, "I shall recite you a song! It has an excellent tune but you will have to take my word for that. It is a drinking song on the excellence of Burgundy wine."

Without further ado, and taking another sip of Burgundy by way of inspiration, he hammered out the words, hammering the table with his fist to add emphasis when necessary:

"My jolly fat host with your face all a-grin,
Come, open the door to us, let us come in.
A score of stout fellows who think it no sin
If they toast till they're hoarse, and they drink till they spin,

Hoofed it amain,
Rain or no rain,
To crack your old jokes, and your bottle to drain.

Such a warmth in the belly that nectar begets
As soon as his guts with its humour he wets,
The miser his gold, and the student his debts,
And the beggar his rags and his hunger forgets.

For there's never a wine
Like this tipple of thine
From the great hill of Nuits to the River of Rhine.

Outside you may hear the great gusts as they go
By Foy, by Duerne, and the hills of Lerraulx,
But the rain he may rain, and the wind he may blow,
If the Devil's above there's good liquor below.

So it abound,
Pass it around,
Burgundy's Burgundy all the year round."

"Bravo!" I cried as he finished, banging the table with the palm of my hands.

"Ah, *la belle France*," he sighed, as he took a further sip of wine.

"Do you know France?" I asked.

"I did."

Yore fell silent, gazing distantly into his wine glass. One could almost touch the memories churning round in his head. I longed for him to tell me about the France he had known.

"No," he whispered, looking up at me, a tear clearly discernable in his eye. "I have wandered too much already.

Sussex is my domain. I have no jurisdiction beyond its borders. It is here that I belong. Or rather it is here that I belonged. Sussex Past. I belong nowhere else."

He smiled: "Tomorrow we shall kiss the Downs."

The Twenty-second of April, 1996

A dull and gloomy morning greeted me as I stepped out of the Bull Hotel. But my mood, which was bright and cheerful, defied it. Come rain or shine, I was determined to enjoy the day's adventure.

My mood brightened further as I spotted Yore standing outside the grocer's shop opposite. Smiling, I crossed the road to join him.

"Chesterton's", he exclaimed as I reached him.

"Pardon?" I asked, surprised at his unorthodox greeting.

"Unorthodox? Certainly not! One can scarcely be more orthodox than Chesterton."

I grinned resignedly. I had no idea what my companion was talking about but, assuming it to be an obscure greeting, I held out my hand in friendship.

"Chesterton's!" I beamed, waiting expectantly for Yore's hand to grasp mine in acceptance.

"No, Chesterton's!" he repeated, his hand ignoring mine but pointing instead to the sign above the shop.

"Oh, Chesterton's", I affirmed, reading the oft-repeated word but still puzzled as to its relevance.

"Good old Chesterton," Yore whispered to himself.

"You know the owner of the shop?" I asked.

"No, I know the owner of the name."

"Chesterton."

"Yes."

"But he doesn't actually own the shop?"

Yore chuckled. "Chesterton. A grocer! Heavens, no! But the shop is named after him. The owner called his shop Chesterton's as a risible response to Chesterton's ' Song Against Grocers'."

"Ah!" I exclaimed triumphantly, "Chesterton is a singer."

Yore laughed heartily. "Chesterton! A singer! He was completely tone deaf! Mind you," he continued, grimacing at the memory, "that didn't stop him singing. If a thing is worth doing at all, he always said, it is worth doing badly. Believe me, Chesterton sang very badly indeed!"

I scratched my head in exasperated bewilderment.

"No," Yore continued, "Chesterton was neither a singer nor a grocer, though he was certainly a Jack of many other trades. He was an essayist, a novelist, a journalist, even a playwright of sorts."

"He was a writer!"

"Not *a* writer. He was one of the greatest writers England has had the honour of nurturing. And, as I forgot to mention, he was also a fine poet. I shall recite the first verse of his 'Song Against Grocers':

> God made the wicked Grocer
> For a mystery and a sign,
> That men might shun the awful shops
> And go to inns to dine;
>
> Where the bacon's on the rafter
> And the wine is in the wood,
> And God that made good laughter
> Has seen that they are good."

"Words of wisdom!" I laughed.

"Indeed," Yore agreed, "but this good Sussex grocer is an honourable exception to the rule. The inn is closed, the grocer's is open. You may buy us some bread and cheese for the journey."

"May I?" I grinned. "Do you have any particular preferences?"

"It must be fully mature English cheddar and the grocer's own, unsliced bread."

"Fine," I chuckled, entering the shop to obey his commands.

Fully provisioned, we set off south towards the Downs. After we had left the road and were walking on a quiet footpath, Yore began to eulogise.

"Do you know this village?" he began. "It has a special place of honour in my county. It is one of the brightest jewels in her crown. One of the brightest and one of the oldest. People have lived here for thousands of years. First there were the flint men, then the Bronze men, then the Celtic Britons. Next came the Romans who built a road right through the village. You know the Bull Hotel where you stayed last night? Well, the road passes a couple of hundred yards to the north of it."

"Really?" I replied, intrigued. "Is any of it still visible?"

"To anyone who knows where to look. Any way, after a couple of centuries of Roman civilisation, the Pax Romana retreated and the barbarians advanced. Dicul and his Saxon folk settled here, giving their name to the village. Dicul is buried beneath the burial mound on Lodge Hill, not far from the Roman road."

As Yore continued his discourse on Ditchling, we reached the foot of the Downs and began to climb steeply. With a briskness which belied his age, Yore set the pace, proceeding with his monologue as he went.

"When St Wilfrid converted the South Saxons to Christianity a small church was built on the site of the present one. The heathen altar stone was removed and is now embedded in the churchyard wall."

"I presume from all this that Ditchling is mentioned in the Domesday Book?"

"Of course," Yore responded dismissively. "The Domesday Book is a work of modern literature as far as Ditchling is concerned. There are written records concerning the village dating from as early as the eighth century. The village passed into the royal hands of King Alfred the Great, who stayed here regularly, and later still to Edward the Confessor. Consequently, the village can claim to have links with two great saints."

"Surely Alfred the Great isn't a saint!" I protested.

Yore smiled. "He hasn't been formally canonised by the Church Militant, if that's what you mean."

"Then he isn't a saint," I insisted.

"Many saints go unrecognised," he replied simply, "but the sin of omission has been forgiven."

We had been climbing steadily and were now almost at the summit of the Downs. We paused and looked back across the village which sprawled prostrate before us.

"Do you see that farm about a mile beyond the church?" Yore continued, pointing to a group of buildings north of the village. "It is the Manor of the Garden. In 1089, William de Warenne, Lord of Lewes, the first Norman to own the vast Ditchling estates, endowed his new monastery at Southover with that large farm. The Manor of the Garden, or Court Gardens Farm as it is now known, fed the monks for 450 years. That is until Henry the Eighth dissolved the monasteries. His henchman, the butcher Thomas Cromwell, was awarded both the monastery at Southover and the Manor of the Garden. But Cromwell, having got rich quick, got poor even quicker. He fell from favour and King Henry had him beheaded. The monastery and the Garden were then handed to Anne of Cleves in return for her not making a fuss over her divorce."

"It all sounds very sordid," I said.

"It was and is," Yore agreed, "but happier times were to return to Ditchling. A little over seventy years ago a group of local artists and craftsmen formed the Guild of St Joseph and St Dominic in Ditchling. The Guild was a society of Catholic craftsmen dedicated to supporting themselves and their families by the practice of a craft. The community flourished and attracted many like-minded people. Another example of good economics."

By now, we had arrived at the summit of Ditchling Beacon. Breathtaking views vied for attention on all sides. Yore drank in a deep draught of the crisp morning air, sank to his knees and kissed the ground ceremoniously.

"High places of Sussex I greet you!"

To the south, rolling hills swept towards the sea. To the north, the whole weald of Sussex spread itself cartologically. To the east, the route of yesterday's journey snaked across the plains as a memorial to our efforts. The pig farm, minuscule and mute in the distance, hid its hideous secret. The picturesque villages of Streat and East Chiltington, retaining their beauty in miniature, conjured up feelings of nostalgia within me even though it was scarcely twelve hours since we had passed through them. The feelings were accentuated by a sudden realisation that I didn't know when, if ever, I would return.

"Come," said Yore. "You are wallowing in the pleasures of Sussex Past when it is time to seek Sussex Present."

Reluctantly, I turned away from the pastoral panorama and followed my companion westward.

"Well, what have we here?" Yore asked suddenly after we had barely walked a hundred yards.

Looking up, I beheld the object of Yore's attention. About thirty yards ahead I saw Yet squatting half-hidden in mud. Only his knees and his body from the chest up were visible.

Yore chuckled. "I urged you to stop wallowing in the pleasures of Sussex Past when we should be looking for Sussex Present, and what do we find? Sussex Future wallowing in Sussex Present!"

"But he doesn't seem to be deriving much pleasure from it," I added as we approached the forlorn figure.

"Mega-avant-garden-powerplay in earnest. Double-plus-ungood!"

As we got closer I saw that Yet was scribbling something onto a small scrap of paper, perched precariously on his knees.

"What are you doing?" I asked, intrigued.

Yet looked up. "Poetry," he said dejectedly. "I'm writing poetry."

"Really?" I said.

"Yes, I find it helps when I am coming down from the magic trips. Poetry helps me sink more slowly."

"May we hear it?" I asked.

"At least it should be good for a laugh," Yore chuckled.

"Avant-garde!" Yet protested. "Poetry is *not* good for a laugh!"

"Oh, you mean your muse doesn't amuse?" Yore quipped mischievously.

"Avant! I don't seek to amuse, I seek to convey the depths of my inner-soul."

"Is it possible to write verse that shallow?"

"What would you know, old man? You are a prisoner of the Past. The Future speaks a language you don't understand."

"Well, let's at least hear what you've written," I interjected.

"Okay, as long as the old man promises not to interrupt."

"I cross my heart," Yore smiled, crossing his heart as he said so.

Yet lifted the scrap of paper a little closer to his face, cleared his throat and began:

"I wandered lonely as a Yard,
So Avant I could cry,
I was really feeling Avant-Garde,
Real Mega-Magpie."

As he finished, I shifted uneasily, unsure of what to say.

Yore was less tactful: "If that is the sound of the Future may the Good Innkeeper call Time before we get there!"

"That," Yet responded cuttingly, "is a great work of Yardish literature. It will win the Post-Poetry Poetry Prize in 2022."

"Will it?" Yore asked incredulously.

"And, what is more, it will be one of the most controversial poems ever written."

"Really?" Yore replied, feigning interest.

"Yes, there will be riots at Sussex University at its

first public recital."

"You don't say," Yore yawned.

"You see, the controversy springs from the failure to employ Yards in the plural. But that, as the philistines at Sussex University failed to realise, is the essential brilliance of the poem. By failing to show Yards the respect it deserves it paradoxically showed it the respect it deserves."

"Does it?" said Yore.

"Pardon?" said I.

"Yes!" Yet exclaimed triumphantly. "By stripping it of its pluralism, it reaffirmed the triumph of pluralism! A Yard on its own is lonely. Hence, Lonely as a Yard. A Yard is an aberration! An abomination! The point is," he continued with renewed excitement, his high-pitched voice reaching a crescendo, "the point is that Yards is Yards, but Yard is Avant-Garde!"

I was totally lost.

Yore had totally lost patience. "What utter rubbish!"

Yet looked hurt. "It is not rubbish, it is the sound of Sussex Future."

"The sound of Sussex Future?" Yore repeated.

"Yes."

"Eh be givene t' Henvul t'mor ter look at dem dere hogs. Dey sey deirm be better dun overn, en sey dey beant. Ouern be a good tot o' shuts an dey be middlin lusty. De travlin's purty bad, and de brooks be out, but b'ou-t-will we shall goo, regn en shall git dere somehow."

"Avant-garde! What was that?"

"That," Yore replied, relishing the moment, "is the sound of Sussex Past!"

"Megamag! Double-plus-ungood! Leave me alone. I need to sleep."

Yet yawned. Elbows on knees, head in hands, he looked a sorry sight.

"Oh, you need to sleep!" Yore exclaimed, as if the realisation had been a revelation.

"Yes," sulked Yet sullenly.

"Then, my dear friend, that is where you're going wrong!"

"Avant! I *need* to sleep."

"No, I mean you have been going wrong by trying to get to sleep by writing when you should have been counting."

"Megamag! Leave me alone!"

"Now, if you only knew the wisdom of the Past you would know that the best way to get to sleep is to count sheep."

"Avant."

"Now, I shall teach you how to count sheep."

"Avant garde! Leave me to rest in peace."

"But if you knew how to count sheep you'd rest in peace a lot more easily."

"I know how to count sheep," Yet yawned, "one, two, three, four. See it's easy. As easy as one-two-three! Now go away!"

"As easy as egdum, pigdum, cockerum, you mean?"

"Magpie! What nonsense is this?"

"It is not nonsense and magpies have nothing to do with it. Mind you, the odd wagtail gets a look in."

"Go away!"

"I think it's best to start with the way the shepherds in my own part of Sussex count their sheep. In West Sussex it's one-e-rum, two-e-rum, cock-e-rum, shu-e-rum, sath-e-rum, winebarrel, wagtail, tarrydiddle, den. Now it's your turn. Repeat after me."

"Magpie!"

"Oh, all right, if you insist. You may say magpie instead of wagtail if you like. But don't let the sheep hear you or you may get the poor things confused."

"Go away!"

"Mind you, the shepherds in the Cuckmere valley count rather differently. One-the-rum, two-the-rum, cau-the-rum, coo-the-rum, sin-the-rum, san-the-rum, winebarrel, jigtarrel, tarrididdle, den. No wagtail, I'm afraid. But you could still say magpie instead of jigtarrel if it would make things easier."

"Mega-avant-garde-powerplay in earnest! Will someone take this madman away!"

"Oh, but I am being rude."

"Yes you are. Now go away!"

"Yes, I've been speaking a strange language which doesn't belong round here. I should have realised that the shepherds from this part of the Downs do it quite differently. Now how does it go?"

"It goes away!"

"Ah yes, I remember. Egdum, pigdum, cockerum, fifer, sizer, corum, withecum, taddle, teedle, den!"

"Avant-garde! If you won't go away then I will. You can count sheep by any archaic language you choose, I'm going to sleep!"

"Good morning and God bless!" Yore quipped chirpily as the top of Yet's head sank gunkingly into the soil of the Downs.

"You see," he continued, turning to me. "Counting sheep. It works every time!"

"I think it was more a case of browbeating him into submission," I countered.

"Or submersion," laughed Yore. "In any case, we must press on. We've been dillydallying or, rather, tarrydiddling for far too long."

Certainly there was to be no dillydallying after the tarrydiddling because Yore strode off at a pace and with a purpose. The purpose, he informed me, was the Plough Inn at Pyecombe, our next port of call.

I wondered, as I struggled to keep up with my companion, whether the superlative speed of his stride was due to any supernatural powers he possessed.

"Are you accusing me of cheating?" he asked plaintively, hearing my thoughts.

"I'm sorry," I said, "I never thought to offend. It's just

that you walk so fast for a man of your, well, age. Come to think of it," I added as an afterthought, "exactly how old are you?"

"Ah!" he said, smiling, "that is a good question."

He strode on in silence.

"If it's a good question, why don't you answer it?"

"A good question deserves a good answer. No, it *demands* a good answer. And I am thinking of the best way to meet the demand."

Accepting his answer, or rather his lack of one, I strode on beside him, bathing in the beauty of the Downs and savouring the serenity of solitude.

The solitude was severed by the long awaited answer.

"I am aged and ageless at one and the same time. In Sufferance I have no age. I dwell in eternity. Mind you, that is not to say that there is no progress in Sufferance. On the contrary, there is nothing but progress in Sufferance. Progress is the whole purpose of Sufferance. The progress of the soul towards Triumph. After the Triumph of the soul, progress is no longer necessary. It is no longer possible. One can't progress beyond perfection."

"Right," I said, utterly bemused and wishing I had never asked the question in the first place.

"I know it's a little difficult to take in," Yore admitted.

"To tell the truth," I complained, "I'm not so sure that I'm not being taken in."

"Taken in?"

"Yes, all this stuff about Sufferance and Triumph. It's a bit far fetched, don't you think?"

"Don't *you* think?" Yore countered.

"Pardon?"

"Don't *you* think?" he repeated.

"Of course I think!"

"Not very deeply obviously. All the great thinkers in history realised the subservience of the subjective self to the objective truth."

"Did they?"

"Yes, but whereas they only *thought* about it in Militance or, if you prefer, in this life, they *know* it in the next. This world asks the questions, the next world answers them."

"Well," I said defiantly, "you still haven't answered *my* question."

Yore looked at me and, as he did so, his countenance lost its sternness.

"I'm sorry," he said. "Patience was never one of my virtues. Believe me, I was trying to answer your question. Not very well perhaps, but then I shouldn't have expected a child to understand pure mathematics. Still less pure metamathematics."

"Oh no, not maths!" I pleaded. "Anything but maths. I *hate* mathematics."

"You shouldn't hate what you don't understand."

"I was speaking metaphorically."

"It's a pity you can't speak metaphysically."

"I think I'm going to be metaphysically sick!"

"You are already metaphysically sick but I hope you are going to be metaphysically cured."

I smiled in exasperation. "I give up! You always have the last word, don't you? Even when the last word is wrong, or it doesn't fit, you have to have it."

Yore returned my smile. "You are right. It's another one of my weaknesses. Even in my previous life in Militance I had to have the last word."

I laughed. "Fine. So be it. But can we *please* change the subject?"

"But I haven't answered your question yet."

"No you haven't. At least we can agree on that!"

"But it was a good question and I should like the opportunity to give you a good answer."

"The trouble is," I said, enjoying my temporary dominance, "that your good answers are always interminably long ones."

"Well," he replied, chuckling, "I do have all the time

in the world."

"And I don't!"

"But I've started so I should like to finish," he pleaded. "And I promise to keep it short."

"You've started so you'll finish," I chuckled. "Okay, Yore, the Ghost of Sussex Past, you have two minutes to answer one question on your specialised subject. Starting . . . now! How old are you?"

Yore was clearly puzzled by my affected manner and choice of words but, after a moment's confused hesitation, he rose to the challenge and endeavoured to answer the question in the two minutes alotted him.

"I have already explained that I am ageless and aged at one and the same time. In Sufferance I dwell in eternity and have no age. However, as part of my progress towards perfection, it was decided by He who Knows Best that I should be incarnated in my Militant body. That which you see before you is he, or me, as he, or I, looked in 1930. In other words, my incarnate self is sixty-years-old."

"Well, for a sixty-year-old you certainly walk fast!" I said, relieved that, at long last, we had finally reached a conclusion.

"Thank you! I was always a good walker. I once held the record for the fastest time between Oxford and London, although that was in my youth."

"That's all very well," I complained, "but is it really necessary to set any speed records now? Can't we take a break?"

"Not until we get to the Plough Inn at Pyecombe. It's not far now."

His last four words came as a great relief because I was weary and in need of a rest. We hadn't walked far but the pace had been exhausting and I almost felt as though we were breaking into a jog on occasions.

Soon we were walking downhill, descending from the Downs to the valley below. We had passed two windmills on our right which Yore informed me were known affectionately as Jack and Jill. Beyond, but out of sight, was the village of Clayton and Yore enthused that the village could boast a history as old as that of Ditchling. People had lived there for at least three thousand years with relics of Bronze Age burials and remains of Roman tiled pavements being unearthed in the area. But Yore saved most of his enthusiasm for Clayton church. It was Saxon, pre-dating the Norman Conquest, and contained wall paintings almost as old as the church itself. Most magnificent of all, he said, was a representation of the Last Judgment over the chancel arch. Yore's enthusiasm was contagious and I almost wished that we could take a diversion to see the church in all its splendour. But I dared not ask. Yore had only one thing on his mind. The Plough Inn at Pyecombe.

We had almost reached the bottom of the steep slope of the Downs before Yore spoke again.

"I have not visited Pyecombe for many years. I don't know how time has treated it. But it will be good to sup at the Plough Inn again."

"I know nothing of Pyecombe," I remarked, "but the prospect of a pint at the Plough is most welcome!"

"Oh, but you must know something of Pyecombe before we get there. It is a fine village. And a notorious one too."

"Notorious?"

"Yes, it was the site of a murder most foul. The murder of George Stonehouse Griffith, a Brighton brewer."

"Why was he killed?" I asked. "Was his beer that bad?"

Yore grinned. "Nobody knows why he was killed. Probably robbery. Nobody knows who killed him. Probably highwaymen. His body was discovered by some men out shooting between Dale Gate and the Plough Inn. An inquest at the inn returned a verdict of wilful murder. Rewards were offered for information leading to the apprehension of the killers but they were never traced. They escaped justice in this life but found it in the next."

"A case of judgment and sentence being deferred" I quipped.

"Quite," Yore agreed, smiling. "But I haven't told you of Pyecombe's greatest claim to fame."

"You haven't," I said, "but I dare say you are going to."

"Indeed, it is not merely a claim to fame but a claim to a place of the highest honour amongst all the villages of holy Sussex."

"Go on," I urged, amused at his hyperbole.

"The heroic deed of the villagers dates back to the time of the Civil War when the good people of Pyecombe outwitted Cromwell and his Prurient troops."

"Surely you mean Puritan troops."

"If I had meant Puritan, I'd have said Puritan. I meant Prurient."

"Fine," I said, puzzled but unwilling to be taken off on another tangent.

"Anyway, as I was saying, Cromwell and his Prurients were descending on the churches of England and desecrating them as they went. In particular, they sought out the beautiful medieval lead fonts which were then melted down to make bullets."

"I suppose that's what is meant by a baptism of fire."

"Very good!" Yore said. "But please let me finish the tale."

"Please do," I said, still laughing at a joke made all the funnier by the satisfying sense that I had beaten Yore at his own game.

"Due to this barbaric practise of melting fonts down to make bullets, there are now only three lead fonts remaining in the whole of Sussex. One is at Edburton. One is at Parham. And the other is here at Pyecombe. How, you may ask, did the Pyecombe font survive the ravages of the Roundheads?"

"Okay then, how *did* the Pyecombe font survive the

ravages of the Roundheads?"

"And the question you may ask is answered by the clue you may see."

"A clue. Where?"

"The clue you may see is on the font itself."

Fortunately, or perhaps deliberately, Yore's procrastination and failure to get to the point, had led us to the gates of Pyecombe church. The gate itself was strange enough, being pivoted in the middle, and Yore took great pleasure in informing me that it was known as a Tapsell gate after the ironmaster at Wadhurst who designed it.

Entering the church, I approached the font with a reverence due more to curiosity than spirituality.

"Can you see anything out of the ordinary?" Yore asked as I peered over it.

"No, I don't think so," I replied.

"The clue is in the flecks of white which are still visible."

"Oh yes!" I exclaimed, my eyes being directed towards white flecks on the font. "But I'm still none the wiser. What does it mean?"

"Precisely. It was a very simple scam but it fooled the simpletons in Cromwell's army as indeed it fooled you. The good villagers of Pyecombe, hearing that there were Prurients in the neighbourhood, and learning from neighbouring villagers what these vandals had done to other churches, decided to protect the font in their own church. They whitewashed it so that it looked like stone! The Prurients arrived, took one look at the font and, believing it was stone, left it where it was. Which is where it still is!"

We left the church and made our way through the village towards the inn. We had only gone a few yards when Yore's attention was drawn towards the notices displayed prominently outside most of the houses. He walked up to one and began reading intently.

"It can't be!" He exclaimed when he had finished.

THE THREE YS MEN

Finding my own interest aroused by his dramatic reaction, I also walked up to the sign. As Yore walked away, stunned by a mixture of apprehension and anger, I read the words on the notice. I soon understood the reason for his exclamation. The national business consortium which owned the Plough Inn was planning to demolish it. In its place they proposed to build a large motel and pleasure complex. The notice expressed the resolute opposition of the villagers who wanted to preserve their village pub. It finished with a request that people should sign a petition calling for the proposals to be scrapped.

When I had read the notice, I followed Yore through the village. He had ambled off ahead, almost shuffling now, the spring in his step exorcised by his changed emotions. I noticed also that nearly every house we passed displayed the same notice prominently. Clearly the consortium had paid no heed to the needs and wishes of the locals when deciding to destroy their local.

I wandered up to Yore as he stood, bemused and bewildered, outside the Plough Inn. It was still there but the reason for his evident disappointment was obvious. The pub itself had been deliberately run down, starved of the investment being saved for the proposed motel. The reason for the motel was also obvious. Cars and lorries roared past in their hundreds. We were on a very busy road, the first busy road I had come across since my daydreaming on London Bridge the previous Friday. Now, as then, I desired to get away from the noise and smell. I gripped my companion lightly but firmly by the elbow and led him towards the entrance of the dilapidated pub. Half-heartedly he resisted, seeming unwilling to enter, but my persistance prevailed and he followed me over the threshold.

"Yo! What kept you!"

Yo! was standing to our left as we entered, dressed in a black t-shirt emblazoned with the logo, "Truckers Rally 1996". He was hand-feeding a flashing fruit-machine with an endless supply of coins.

"Hi, Yo!", I replied, genuinely pleased to see him. His manically smiling face lightened the load of the gloom-laden mood into which Yore and I had slipped. At least it lightened my load. It had scarcely lightened Yore's who had slumped disconsolately on a bench in the corner.

"Want a go?" he asked, stepping back from the machine to allow me to feed it.

"No thanks, I don't."

Yo! shrugged. "You don't do much, do you?"

"I drink sometimes," I replied. "Do you want one?"

"Yo! Straight orange!"

"You want orange juice?" I asked above the noise of the flasher regurgitating some of the excess coins it had been fed.

"Yo! No! Straight orange! That's a tenner!"

Yo! genuflected before the flasher in order to scoop the tokens from its mouth.

"Right," I said, feigning interest. "But would you like a drink?"

"Yo! A bunch of fives!"

I waited expectantly for the flasher to regurgitate some more of its lunch, but the machine remained silent.

"Evidently a bunch of fives isn't as good as a straight orange," I remarked.

Yo! laughed. "No! A straight orange wins a tenner. A bunch of fives costs about two quid."

"That's too bad," I said. "But what would you like to drink?"

"Yo! A bunch of fives!" Yo! repeated, roaring with laughter. "A bunch of fives is a drink!"

"Is it?" I asked, confused. "What is it?"

"It's brill! Five different flavours. Mango, lime, passion fruit, banana and bubble gum. A bunch of fives! And it's eight per cent alcohol. Wicked! Sweet as a nut and'll blow yer brains!"

I grinned and shook my head. As I wouldn't describe myself as sweet, or a nut, and as I had no particular desire to blow my brains, I resolved to stick to good old-fashioned ale. I expected Yore to join me but, still silent and pensive in the corner, he waved me away dismissively when I approached.

Oh well, I thought, at least it's going to be a cheap round. One bunch of fives and a single pint of ale. The bunch of fives was simple enough. Upon being asked, the woman behind the bar placed a garish turquoise can in front of me. It was decorated with the caricatured face of a designer-ugly yob and underneath were the words "sweet as a nut and'll blow yer brain". I smiled. Yo! gets zero for originality, I thought, and less for taste.

Now my difficulties began. It was easy enough to buy any of a whole range of the new high-powered chemical mixtures favoured by Yo!, but a traditional pint of ale posed a greater problem.

I recognised the names of the beers on offer. They were all well-known national brands sold through the power of advertising. But, as far as I was concerned, they were not so much famous as infamous. At best, bland. At worst, downright undrinkable. I chose what I thought would be the least noxious, but the first sip proved me wrong. It was awful! Grimacing, I returned to Yo! and presented him with the ice-cold can.

"Yo!" he said.

"You're welcome," I replied.

"Is he?" Yo! asked, nodding in the direction of the sullen black mass in the corner. "What's got in to him?"

"It's more a case of he's got in to here," I replied.

"Not his sort of pub?"

"It was, but it isn't now."

"It isn't now because it's been murdered," the black mass interjected.

"Murdered!" Yo! scoffed. "How can anyone murder a pub?"

"It is not *a* pub. It is the Plough Inn at Pyecombe. The soul of Sussex breathed life into it for centuries. But now it is dead. Murdered. All that remains is a tomb containing the ghosts of those generations of Sussex men who passed through here. And," he continued, looking around him at the decaying decor, "I am one of the ghosts."

"Then why don't you rest in peace, old man?"

"Only the angels and the Triumphant souls rest in peace. All the rest are restless."

"This is too much!" Yo! exploded. "I can't stand any more of your Triumphalist nonsense!"

"You can't escape from Divine Symmetry."

"To hell with Divine Symmetry!"

"Hell is the result of Divine Symmetry. Mind you," he added, grinning like the Grim Reaper, "our present situation could be the result of diabolical symmetry. If you had said 'to hell with diabolical symmetry' I would have agreed with you."

"Diabolical symmetry. That's a new one!"

"Hardly new, my dear Present. It's as old as Hell itself. Though it's new to you. But then," he quipped, chuckling mischievously, his spirits lifting slightly, "everything is new to you, isn't it? Or at least it would be if you were honest enough to stick to your principles. As it is, of course, you are always borrowiing from the Past, half understanding old ideas, or abusing them, so that they change or lose all meaning."

"At least," Yo! countered, "I am not trapped in the Past and condemned to keep repeating the same old mistakes."

"It is not being condemned to the Past that you should worry about, but being condemned in the Future. Which," Yore said, smiling, "brings us back to diabolical symmetry."

"I feared as much," I muttered.

"Yo!" said Yo!, agreeing with me.

"Yes," continued Yore, undeterred. "The Plough Inn is the victim of diabolical symmetry."

"God help us," I groaned.

"Quite," said Yore. "Now, if you'll allow me to continue."

"Do we have any choice?"

"Yo!"

"I think," Yore continued, answering my question by ignoring it, "that the destruction of this fine old inn is the work of the Devil himself."

"The Devil!" Yo! remarked in ridicule. "So the developers have nothing to do with it, I suppose?"

"Of course they have something to do with it. They are doing the Devil's work."

"I'm sure that's a *non sequitur*," I said.

"Not to mention an *argumentum ad hominem*," Yo! added.

Yore smiled but brushed the objections aside. "If it is true that the Devil finds work for idle hands, which it is, it is even more true that he finds work for greedy hands."

Yo! grinned, a menacing gleam in his eye. "If it were true that the Devil existed, which it isn't, you would have a point, which you don't. Your argument falls down on first principles."

"On the contrary," Yore countered, "*he* fell by the rejection of first principles."

"What?"

"Or, to be more precise, he fell by the rejection of *the* first principle."

"Who?"

"The Devil."

"This is ridiculous!"

"And you, my dear Present, have repeated his mistake. My argument stands by the acceptance of first principles. Your argument falls by their rejection."

"Absurd."

"And now you have fallen into an *argumentum ad absurdum*."

"Touche!" Yo! laughed.

"Of course, the Devil's real name is He who Hates.

And you know what he hates more than anything else?"

Yore paused for either member of his audience to reply but, failing to elicit a response, he continued.

"What he hates more than anything else is to lose an argument. And that is why his argument with He who Loves will continue until the end of time."

"I'm not so sure that this isn't going to run it a close second," I complained.

"Yo!" Yo! assented.

Yore beamed apologetically. "I'm sorry. I digressed again."

"Yes you did," I confirmed.

"But any way," he continued, "all this brings us back to the destruction of the Plough Inn."

"Does it?" Yo! asked incredulously.

"How?" I queried.

"Because it is one of the Devil's jokes. It is a bad joke of course. All his jokes are bad jokes. But it is not unamusing in a nasty sort of way."

"If it is a joke, will you please get to the punch line!" I demanded impatiently.

"And put us out of our misery," Yo! complained.

"Ah, but the Devil's jokes always put people into misery," Yore quipped.

"Get to the point!"

"Well, do you remember the story I told you about the murder of George Stonehouse Griffith, the Brighton brewer?"

"Yes."

"And you remember that the inquest against the killers was held here at the Plough Inn?"

"Yes."

"But did you know that Griffith's company, the Rock Brewery, was taken over during my worldly life by the company that now owns this inn?"

"No I didn't. So?"

"Don't you see? It's the Devil's final revenge on this

inn for its paying host to those who passed judgment against his disciples who murdered the brewer all those years ago."

"How?"

"Diabolical symmetry. The Devil's disciples murder the brewer. The Plough passes judgment on the murderers. The Devil curses the Plough. The brewer's brewery is then laid waste by a bigger brewery. The bigger brewery then lays waste to the Inn of justice. The Devil's curse prevails. A diabolical joke, rejoicing in the victory of murder and waste over justice."

"You were right about one thing," I said when he had finally finished, "it was certainly a diabolical joke. One of the worst I've ever heard. It wasn't even funny."

"But I'm sure the Devil found it hilarious," Yore replied. "He has a strange sense of humour. Even now I imagine that the pits of Hell are ringing to the sound of diabolical laughter."

"And talking of the pits," I remarked, pushing away my unfinished pint, "can we please get out of this place?"

"Yo!"

"Yes," Yore sighed, taking one last, lingering look at the Plough's rotting remains.

Passing into the car park outside the pub, we were struck instantly by the din of traffic.

"Where now?" I asked above the noise.

"Over the brow of West Hill and down the other side into Saddlescombe," Yore replied, pointing south-west towards a track, clearly discernible as a grey stripe up the side of the next hill.

Although the track commenced from the other side of the road, about twenty yards away, there was a seemingly insurmountable barrier. Between it and us was the A23, the main London to Brighton road. It was protected from the feet of pedestrians by a high fence and, in any case, there was a solid wall of speeding cars and lorries. To cross would be to dice with death.

"How do we get across?" I said, asking the obvious question.

"We walk!" Yore replied angrily.

"How?"

"Straight across!"

"Don't be stupid!" I exclaimed.

"Yo!" said Yo!, enjoying our altercation and the dilemma we faced.

"We have the right of way," Yore affirmed.

"No we don't! It's a dual carriageway!"

"Men have *walked* the South Downs Way for thousands of years, long before infernos were ever thought of. Therefore, by the laws of tradition and precedent *we* have the right of way."

"You're mad!"

"It's taken you long enough to realise!" exclaimed Yo!, laughing more loudly than ever. "By the way, old man, is that your proper surname. Mad. It fits you very well. Yore Mad!"

"No," Yore continued, oblivious to Yo!'s jibes, "there is nothing else for it. We must part the waves and pass across to the other side."

He started forward towards the barriers at the side of the dual carriageway. Panic-stricken, I pulled him back.

"Yore! Stop! You'll cause an accident!"

"Accidents must always give way to essentials."

I didn't understand his answer but I knew that the only essential thing at the moment was to prevent Yore's suicidal intentions.

"But we could get killed!" I shouted.

"I can't get killed," he replied.

"But I can!" I screamed angrily.

"Which is why I shall stop the infernos so that you can cross safely."

Shrugging off my restraining grip on his sleeve, he made briskly and resolutely for the barrier.

"You're mad!" I screamed.

THE THREE YS MEN

"Yore Mad!" Yo! repeated mockingly.

Within seconds Yore scaled the barrier and strode out into the path of oncoming traffic. He stood there, jaw jutted out defiantly, right hand raised authoritively, facing a huge juggernaut which roared towards him at speed.

"Oh my God!" I squealed hysterically. "It's not going to stop!"

Several tons of metal careered into Yore at sixty miles an hour.

"He's history," Yo! chuckled tastelessly. Amazingly, as the lorry sped on without even braking, Yore stood rooted to the same spot, apparently unhurt. A little shaken perhaps, but essentially unharmed by his experience.

"Look out!" I shouted.

Too late. A Peugeot 205 sped through him at seventy miles an hour. Confused, bemused and disorientated, he dusted himself down, dodged other traffic, and beat a hasty retreat. Dejectedly he climbed back over the barrier and returned to us. He looked dishevelled, as though he had spent the night on a park bench.

Yo! was doubled up, creased with laughter and guffawing uncontrollably.

I didn't know whether to laugh or cry. Above all, I was overwhelmingly relieved that no-one had been hurt.

"Well, Yore Mad," Yo! began between laughs, "let that be a lesson to you. You can't stop progress!"

"It isn't progress," Yore sulked defiantly.

Yo! creased up again. "Well that truck found no problem progressing through you!"

"It never progressed. It proceeded."

"Either way," I remarked, "it was a pretty stupid thing to do."

"Yeah," Yo! agreed, "real dumb!"

"Yes it was stupid," Yore conceded contritely.

"As stupid as King Canute trying to stop the tide coming in!" Yo! jibed, thoroughly enjoying his adversary's downfall.

"You do an injustice to Canute," Yore replied sadly. "He was a wise and just king and would never have been as foolish as I."

"But he was," Yo! protested. "He stood on the beach ordering the tide not to come in. You can't get much dumber than that!"

"It was an act of wisdom," Yore insisted, his eyes downcast, dejected.

"Like trying to stop the traffic on the A23!"

"No, as I said, King Canute would never have been so foolish."

"But he was!"

"He wasn't. He was pointing out the foolishness of others. His courtiers, wishing to curry favour, flattered him by saying that he was such a mighty king that even the tide would obey him. Canute, to prove them wrong, had his throne carried onto the beach where he carried out a scientific experiment. He got his feet wet and, in so doing, proved that there was a Power in the Universe greater than he."

"Thanks for the history lesson," I interjected, "but exactly how are we to get across this road?"

"Go on, have another go!" Yo! mocked. "You may get run over by a bus this time!"

Yore, ignoring the taunts, lowered his eyes to the ground for a few moments. Presently he looked up, sighed deeply, and spoke.

"In penance I shall take the pedars way."

"But that's in Norfolk!" I protested.

"Hardly," replied Yore solemnly, "but it is north."

Looking up the road, he pointed to a bridge about four hundred yards away.

"That is the pedars way, it is the only way pedars are allowed to pass these days. The infernos have won."

"Why don't you thumb a lift, it's quicker!" scoffed Yo!

"Why don't you . . ." Yore's words tailed off as his

attention was caught by an electric blue blob speeding towards him. The blob was unmistakable. Yet, waving frantically, sat astride the roof of a lorry which was cruising north towards them.

"Yo!" said Yo!, holding out his thumb, "I think my lift has just arrived."

"Yards!" cried Yet, swooping down from the top of the lorry, scooping Yo! up in one swing of his arms, and remounting the roof.

The two sped off northwards, leaping over the bridge Yore had pointed out as though it were a hurdle, and landing safely back on top of the lorry. Within seconds they were out of sight.

I was alone once more with Yore. We plodded slowly towards the same bridge, oppressed by the noise of traffic, and crossed it. We then plodded back again on the other side of the road until we picked up the track opposite the Plough. It wasn't until we were halfway up West Hill, with the sound of the road subsiding to nothing more than the irritating drone of a mosquito, that we spoke again.

"Tell me," I said, "why did that lorry pass straight through you?"

"Because I was foolish and exceeded the limits of my jurisdiction."

"I don't understand. You said you could be seen. I could feel you when I pulled you back by the sleeve. It doesn't make sense."

"Oh but it does. Remember when Present arrived on the back of Future at the equestrian centre?"

"Yes."

"And I said he could never be seen when he behaved outrageously."

"Yes," I said, remembering the conversation following Yo! and Yet's Wagnerian entrance. "But you told me that you could be seen."

"Yes, and so can Present under normal circumstances. Past and Present are always visible to this world. Only the

Future remains invisible."

"But that lorry passed straight through you without even braking. He couldn't have seen you."

"He didn't. I had made the same mistake as Present. I had behaved in a way which exceeded my rights in this world. I have no right to behave irresponsibly. Nor has Present. But Present is often irresponsible and blind to the consequences of his actions. That is why He who Faced the Consequences ensures that the world is blind to the consequences of Yo!'s actions."

I scratched my head. It was all a bit much to take in.

Yore continued. "But *I* should know better. I am older and I should have learned from the mistakes of the past. I had no right to interfere with the infernos. I allowed my anger to cloud my judgment. I was wrong, so He who Sees Everything ensured that I could not be seen."

I scratched my head again. It still didn't make sense.

"But *I* could see you. Even when you stood in front of the traffic. And I can see Yo! even when he is behaving outrageously. And I can see Yet who is always invisible."

Yore smiled. "That's because you have been given a gift. You have been made a Seer for the purposes of this journey across my county. Past, Present and Future. We are all here to guide you."

"Why?"

"So that you may attain Wisdom."

"Why me?"

"Why not?"

I was still hopelessly confused but I gained a strange sort of solace from Yore's last answer, even if it was in the form of a question. I am here therefore I am. Why not!

During our conversation we had passed over the brow of West Hill and were descending steeply into Saddlescombe. Within minutes we had left the tiny hamlet behind us and were climbing the next hill.

I felt at peace with my surroundings and in communion with nature itself. By now our uphill trek had taken us into lightly wooded country. The sound of birdsong filled the air and high above I spied a bird of prey circling methodically.

"Is that a kestrel?" I asked.

"No, a sparrowhawk," Yore replied, gazing up at the gliding raptor.

"Beautiful, isn't it?"

"Not if you happen to be a sparrow or a blue tit," Yore said, smiling. Then, grinning more broadly, he added: "But then a sparrow or a blue tit have no conception or perception of beauty any way!"

"It's funny," I continued, ignoring his philosophical aside, "you don't think of the prey when you think of a bird of prey, do you?"

"That's because one only sees the silent gliding or hovering and seldom the swoop and kill."

True, I thought, recalling the dozens of times I had seen kestrels hovering without ever seeing them swoop.

"Take the sparrowhawk," Yore continued. "It is a ruthlessly efficient killer. Its victim never hears or sees anything. Its presence is felt only after it silently sweeps down to strike. Then, once the three-cornered carnivore has grabbed its prey, feathers fly and that's that. Or, rather, that isn't that as far as the hapless victim is concerned. A sparrowhawk eats its prey alive. All that is required of its victim is that it should stay still while being dismembered sliver by sliver."

I grimaced. "Gruesome!"

We continued to climb, skirting the edge of the wood. To our right I noticed a deep, steep-sided gully gashing the terrain.

"Devil's Dyke," Yore announced, hearing my thoughts. "It was another one of the Devil's pranks, or at least that's the way legend has it. He was so jealous of holy Sussex that he dug the dyke through the middle of the Downs so that the Weald would be flooded by the sea. Unfortunately for the Devil, but fortunately for Sussex, St

THE THREE YS MEN

Dunstan got to hear of his dastardly deed and foiled him before he finished the job."

I gave my companion a sarcastic look.

"A dyke dug by the Devil! That's the silliest story you've told me yet!"

Yore smiled. "It's a good story. But I will confess that I don't believe it to be factual."

"Good," I replied, relieved that he wasn't expecting me to believe his crazy tale.

Yore grinned mischievously. "Not factual, but true."

"Oh come on!" I exclaimed in exasperation.

In spite of my protestation, Yore continued.

"As with all good legends, the story is only a means to an end. The facts of the story aren't as important as the truth it contains."

"Are you expecting me to believe that this dyke was dug by the Devil?"

"No, that is the irrelevant part related to the alleged facts. It is the truth of the legend that matters."

"The truth?"

"Yes, the truth is that the Devil would like to destroy Sussex, if he could, and the reason he has failed to do so is the intercession of St Dunstan."

"Right," I muttered, baffled by his train of thought.

"You think I am being illogical, don't you?"

I didn't reply, but my grin and the glint in my eye confirmed his suspicions.

"I am being strictly logical. Take those trees, for instance. The facts will tell us how they grew but they can't tell us why they grew. Only the truth can tell us why trees exist. And the truth resides in the Mind of the Tree Maker."

"Be that as it may," I countered, "the truth about Devil's Dyke is not so much logical as geological."

"Heresy!" Yore asserted. "The facts about Devil's Dyke are geological. The truth is theological!"

"Why?"

"Precisely," said Yore.

"Pardon?"

"Why is Devil's Dyke? is a theological question. How is Devil's Dyke? is a geological question. The first explains the truth. The second explains the facts. The truth is the end. The facts are the means to the end."

"I still don't get you."

Yore sighed.

"Let's start at the very beginning," he began. "In the beginning Sussex didn't exist. It was only an idea in the Mind of the Great Sculptor. A very good idea, one of the best He's ever had, but only an idea none the less. Having decided to mould Sussex in his own image, the Sculptor had to decide *how* he was going to do this. Finally he decided to write the laws of Geology by which Sussex could be built. So you see, Sussex was the end of his efforts, the 'why', and geology was the means to the end, the 'how'."

"I see," I said, only half telling the truth because I only half understood it. But although I wasn't sure that I understood, I was sure that I had no desire for the ontological discussion to continue.

We had left Devil's Dyke behind us and had reached the top of the hill. Breath-taking views of the Sussex weald greeted us. I drank them in thirstily, quenching myself with beauty.

"This calls for bread and cheese!" Yore exclaimed, sitting on the grass. I joined him and removed from the bag the provisions I had bought at Chesterton's that morning. Breaking a large chunk of bread from the loaf, I handed it to my companion. Then, dividing the cheese into two roughly equal blocks, I passed one to Yore who muttered a short prayer in Latin, crossed himself and began to eat. Hungrily, I took my first bite of the mature cheddar. It was delectable, complementing perfectly the view before us, a panorama that encompassed and embraced mile upon mile of flat, rural wealden countryside.

After several minutes silent contemplation, Yore drew

my attention to the village nestling at the foot of the Downs, about a mile distant.

"See that village," he began, "it boasts a fine inn, the Dog and Shepherd, so-called because it stands beside a freshwater spring which once made the village a centre for sheep washing. Fulking! It's a lovely place. Flintstone cottages overshadowed precipitously by the glory of the Downs."

"Sounds idyllic," I agreed.

"Not quite. It lacks only one thing. A church. The nearest is at Edburton, a mile or so further west. The church there was founded by Edburgh, King Alfred's daughter."

Reluctantly, having devoured the last of our bread and cheese, we rose. I was thirsty and, having been cheated of a drinkable beer at the Plough, I was tempted by the prospect of a pint at the Dog and Shepherd in Fulking. My guide, however, had other ideas. He strode out westward, following the roof of the Downs. We climbed over Edburton Hill and Truleigh Hill, passing ancient tumuli and being welcomed at every turn by new and glorious views. From the top of Truleigh Hill, Yore pointed out an impressive structure five miles to the south west in the Vale of Adur. It was, he informed me, Lancing College Chapel, built in Victorian times but in the style of thirteenth century gothic. Although too far away for the discernment of detail, the power of the imagination magnified its beauty. Magnificence in miniature.

Looking down on this world of miniatures from the sanctuary of solitude on the rural roof of Sussex, I was overcome by a tranquility seldom attainable in life's hustle and bustle. I was like a god looking down on the world below and seeing that it was good. The Downs were, I decided, not only a piece of Sussex but the very peace of Sussex. A heaven haven.

After Truleigh Hill we began to descend into the groove carved through the Downs by the River Adur. Soon the distant drone of cars heralded the end of our sojourn with silence, an uncivil reminder of the approach of civilisation.

"We shall not go on," said Yore as we reached the brow of Beeding Hill. "There is another main road ahead and I shan't cross another today."

He smiled reassuringly and then continued.

"We can go down into Upper Beeding, cross the Adur, pass through Bramber and so reach the Chequers in Steyning."

Following the route he prescribed, Yore bestowed his extensive historical learning on me as we went. It was thus that I learned that Upper Beeding meant the upper place of prayer and that it had been home to the Benedictines. I learned also that Bramber had been one of the most important towns in Sussex during Saxon times but was now no more than a village. Its castle, built by the Normans to guard the gap in the Downs from foreign invasion, was destroyed by Cromwell's Roundheads. Steyning, our final destination, had been a major port until the Adur silted up in the fourteenth century.

Finally, we reached the Chequers inn. Ordering two pints of Arundel Best bitter, I sat down and felt the blood rushing to my feet in an ecstasy of thanksgiving. Bliss! The day's labour was over and I supped my ale in celebration. Taste buds responded and I was pleasantly surprised by the full, pungent, wood-smoke flavour. Locally brewed ale of the highest quality!

I was hungry also but my hunger could wait. I would eat later. For the moment I would drink!

The Twenty-third of April, 1996

It was a misty, miserable morning when I met my guide outside the Chequers Inn. He was, as ever, dressed in the same sombre black broadcloth and I considered how the dullness of his clothes matched the dullness of the day. On this particular morning, however, a small splash of white adorned his collar. A rose.

"Happy Holy Day!" he exclaimed brightly upon my arrival.

"Holiday?" I queried.

"Yes! Happy Holy Day!"

I looked puzzled.

"Don't you know what day it is?" he asked.

I thought for a moment. I had lost track.

"Tuesday," I replied.

"Tuesday!" he snapped contemptuously, "and you call yourself an Englishman?"

"Pardon?"

He looked to the heavens in exasperation.

"What is today?" he asked again.

I stared at him blankly.

"Today's date," he repeated. "What is the date today?"

I thought again. "April the twenty-third."

"So?" he prompted.

"So what?" I asked.

"So it's the Feast Day of England's patron saint, St George!"

"Oh, St George's Day!" I exclaimed.

"Precisely."

"Is that why you're wearing the rose?"

"Of course."

"But shouldn't it be red?" He sighed.

"Alas, it is true that England's rose is traditionally red, but I can't bring myself to wear a red rose."

"Why?" I asked, intrigued.

"Because it is indelibly stained with the blood-letting

of the Tudors."

"I don't understand."

"The red rose of Lancaster."

"Pardon?"

He sighed deeply again and then smiled.

"It doesn't matter really. Let's just say that I am an old man who never forgets. I forgive, or at least I try to, but I can't forget. For me the Tudor rose is stained with the blood of the English Martyrs. I cannot see a blood red rose without thinking of the crimes of Henry the Eighth and Bloody Bess."

"I see," I said uncertainly.

"But now," he said chirpily, "the blood they spilled has washed the heavenly souls of the English Martyrs whiter than snow. Which is why I wear a white rose on St George's Day."

"Right," I said.

All the while Yore had been indulging his botanical pedantry we had been walking westward. We had left the last remaining dwellings of Steyning behind us and, joining a footpath, began the steep climb back onto the roof of the Downs. Pausing about half-way up we admired the aerial view of the town we had stayed in. Shrouded in mist it was barely visible but looked the more impressive for the mysterious veil with which the morning had clothed it.

"You know," said Yore, "although it is the Feast of St George, I am sure he won't mind if I sing the praises of the holy saint of Steyning."

"Who?"

"The holy saint of Steyning. St Cuthman."

"Never heard of him," I muttered dismissively.

"Oh, but you must," Yore insisted. "It would be a sin if you were to pass through this holy part of my county without becoming acquainted with her greatest saint."

"Yo!"

Startled by the interruption, Yore and I looked up. Above us towered Yo! standing on top of the triangulation point which surmounts Steyning Round Hill.

"I'm the king of the castle and Yore the dirty rascal!" he chanted childishly.

"From the sublime to the ridiculous," muttered Yore.

"More like the sublime to the cor blimey!" I replied.

"Yo!" said Yo!.

"Yo!" said I.

"What's happening?" Yo! rapped in his best ghetto American.

"Before you rudely interrupted me," Yore responded tersely, "I was about to recount the story of St Cuthman."

"Saints!" Yo! protested. "What earthly relevance have saints to the twentieth century!"

"Their earthly relevance," Yore retorted, "is linked to their heavenly presence."

"Superstitious garbage!"

"And, of course, by heavenly presence I mean both their presence in Heaven and their heavenly presence on earth."

"Trash! Complete garbage."

"No," replied Yore impishly, "there is no trash in heaven, to use your Yankeeism, the trash goes elsewhere."

"Please!" I pleaded. "No more!"

"Yo!" said Yo!

"Then," Yore continued, "may we get back to St Cuthman?"

"No!" said Yo!

"Yes," said I, "but *please* keep to the point and *try* not to wander off the subject."

"I shall and I will," Yore grinned, "but we must walk as we talk. We have many miles to travel before we reach the Cricketers in Duncton, the inn where we shall spend the night."

"Okay," I said. "Yo! are you coming with us?"

Yo! looked disapprovingly at the sky.

"I don't know. It looks like rain."

I also looked skywards. He was right. It did.

"Yo!," Yo! continued, "but I'll come along with you for a short while. In any case, I'm looking for Yet. Have you seen him?"

"Not since we saw him with you on the A23."

"Yo! That was real wild! Wicked! Mega-cool!"

He leapt effortlessly from the obelisk upon which he'd been perched and began walking beside us.

Yore then recited the story of St Cuthman, an eighth century saint who was born at Chidham, near Bosham, but lived and preached in Steyning. According to Yore he was the St Francis of Sussex, living in poverty all his life, teaching the gospel of peace, and building the first church in Steyning with his own hands.

"And," Yore continued, concluding his tale, "St Cuthman should be the patron saint of all devoted sons. From the moment his father died, he looked after his paralysed mother, pulling her in a cart everywhere he went."

"What a weirdo!" Yo! scoffed, laughing. "He must have looked really stupid dragging his mum around."

At that moment it started to rain. And as it it started to rain Yore started to laugh. Soon he was guffawing so noisily that it drowned and then silenced Yo!'s derisive laughter.

"What's so funny?" Yo! asked, rain dripping from the end of his nose.

"Laugh men," Yore began between bouts of uncontrollable laughter. "Laugh men, weep Heaven!"

"What?"

Yore composed himself sufficiently to continue, chuckling as he did so.

"St Cuthman's prayer. Laugh men, weep Heaven."

"I don't get it?"

"Then, my dear Present, I shall explain. When St Cuthman first arrived at Steyning, pulling his mother in the cart, the rope over his shoulder broke and his mother was thrown out onto the road. While he was struggling to get her back into the cart, some men and women mowing hay in a field started to laugh at their predicament. St Cuthman called out to them 'Laugh men, weep Heaven' and immediately there was a great deluge, ruining the crop. And ever since then, so the local folk maintain, it always rained whenever Penfold's field was being mown."

"What superstitious trash!" Yo! exclaimed when Yore had finished. "No wonder this part of the world was known as Silly Sussex."

"When Sussex was called Silly," Yore retorted, "it was taken as a compliment and considered an honour."

"Really?" laughed Yo!, "you can't get much sillier than that!"

"I see, dear Present, that you are in need of an English lesson."

"I don't think so."

"I do."

"There is nothing wrong with my English," Yo! insisted.

"Everything is wrong with your English."

"Why?"

"Because you can't speak it."

"I speak very good English."

"You speak very bad American."

"Get real!" Yo! protested.

"Exactly," Yore smiled, "but I'd rather get silly."

"What?"

"Silly."

"This conversation is silly!" I complained, losing patience with the impasse.

"The point is," said Yore, finally getting to it, "that Present here believes 'silly' to be a term of abuse because he doesn't know the true meaning of the word."

"*You're* silly," said Yo!

"Thank you," said Yore.

"By which I mean you are stupid, ignorant and dumb."

"Then I can't be silly," Yore smiled.
"Don't be silly!" Yo! exclaimed.
"Make up your mind!" said Yore.
"This is getting us nowhere," I interjected plaintively.

"Let me explain," continued Yore. "The word 'silly' comes from the old English word *'saelig'*, which means innocence, or happiness, even holiness in some circumstances. Therefore, when Sussex in happier times was known as Silly Sussex it was a term of endearment, worthy of admiration and respect. Silly Sussex was Happy Sussex or Holy Sussex. May she become silly again!"

I could see that Yo! was far from happy with Yore's explanation but he seemed content to let the matter rest.

We continued to walk, following the chalky path of the South Downs Way as it wended its way north-west. Far below on the weald I could make out through the damp murk an old house set in extensive gardens.

"Wiston House and Park," Yore informed me.

Unusually, however, he seemed reluctant to say more, but chose instead to discuss an old farmhouse beyond the Park.

"Wiston House is a well-known landmark, an Elizabethan mansion," he said simply, "but beyond its grounds lies a hidden jewel, Buncton Manor."

Although Yore pointed in the direction of his hidden jewel, it was not discernible through the drizzly mist. The jewel remained hidden.

But if its attractiveness could not be apprehended visually, Yore could at least praise it verbally. For a minute or so he waxed lyrical.

"To the untrained eye Buncton Manor looks like any old farmhouse. But the eye, particularly the untrained eye, can be deceived. The current building is five hundred years old but its roots stretch back far further. The Domesday record made in 1086 showed its Saxon roots. Indeed, its name is derived from 'the people of Buna' who settled there on an enclosed farm, or 'tun', at the time of the first Saxon invasions, after the Romans left, in about the year 500. So, you see, Buncton Manor is as old as the earliest South Saxons who gave their name to my county."

"Big deal," muttered Yo!, disgruntled.

"I take it you are not enjoying yourself," I asked.

"Enjoying myself!" Yo! complained. "It's raining. I'm getting wet. Miles from civilisation. On top of some hill. Bored out of my brains. No, I am *not* enjoying myself!"

"I see," I said.

"Why don't you take a trip to Brighton?" Yore suggested. "There's bound to be enough vulgarity there to keep you amused."

"Because," Yo! snapped, "I am supposed to be taking a trip with Yet."

"Ah!" exclaimed Yore knowingly, "you were supposed to be meeting him this morning."

"Yes, but he hasn't shown up."

"Not shown up Yet," Yore chuckled. "Perhaps that should be his nickname. Notshownup Yet!"

"Very funny," Yo! moaned. Then, as an afterthought, "I could kill him sometimes. He's so unreliable."

"The Future is always unreliable," Yore said sagely.

"Possibly," Yo! retorted, "but he's a lot more fun than the boring old Past!"

"For the Present, dear Present, it appears that the boring old Past is all you have!"

Yo! grunted grudgingly.

"And talking of the boring old past," Yore continued, "we are coming to possibly the most famous landmark in the whole of Sussex. Chanctonbury Ring."

"I've heard of that, I think," I said. "What is it?"

"Ah! That's a good question," enthused Yore, warming visibly to his subject. "Today most people know it as a circle of beech trees on top of the Downs."

"What's so exciting about a circle of trees?" scoffed Yo!

"Nothing is exciting to a cynic," Yore replied. "A

cynic has lost the ability to feel excitement. He is emotionally handicapped."

"It's still only a circle of trees," Yo! insisted.

"It is not *only* a circle of trees, but even if it was it would have an intrinsic beauty."

"If you are into trees."

"If you are into beauty."

"Okay, okay," I interrupted in my role as referee and peacemaker, "the point is, what makes this particular circle of trees so famous?"

"First," Yore began as we stopped at the Ring's perimeter, "because the circle can be seen from many parts of my county and many places outside my county in the No Man's Land beyond its borders. It is visible from the London to Brighton railway line, north of Clayton, from Butser Hill in Hampshire and from Leith Hill in Surrey. It is the wooded crown of the Downs, trumpeting her majesty throughout the South Country. Sadly, the crown was badly damaged during the great hurricane of October 1987, but even as a shadow of her former self the Ring is beautiful."

"How old is the Ring?" I asked, finding Yore's enthusiasm contagious.

"Another good question!" Yore bubbled. "It depends."

"Depends on what?"

"On what you call the Ring."

"Sorry?"

"The Ring," Yore repeated. "The Ring of Beech trees is not very old but they were planted inside the perimeter of an Iron Age hillfort which also contains the remains of a Roman Temple, and a Celtic temple even older still."

"Fantastic!" I exclaimed with added interest.

"A heap of ruins with trees on top," said Yo! dismissively.

"The trees were planted over two hundred years ago by Charles Goring who lived in Wiston House. As he was a mere youth when he planted them, only nineteen-years-old, and as he lived well into his eighties, he had the good fortune to see the beeches grow to full maturity. When he was an old man he wrote a poem about the Ring which, as I happen to know it by heart, I shall recite to you:

> How oft around thy Ring, sweet Hill,
> A boy, I used to play,
> And form my plans to plant thy top
> On some auspicious day . . .
> With what delight I placed those twigs
> Beneath thy maiden sod;
> And then an almost hopeless wail
> Would creep within my breast.
> Oh! could I live to see thy top
> In all its beauty dress'd.

He died a happy man because his wish was granted."

Yore fell silent for awhile, deep in thought. As he did so, I looked round the circle from its centre. It was strange. Spooky. Whether the weather was the cause I couldn't say, but certainly the murkiness added mystery to the place. Spirits of ages past seemed to swirl in and out of the gloom between the branches of the beech trees. I was glad I wasn't alone.

Presently, Yore resumed his history of the Ring.

"The Ring's earlier history is shrouded in uncertainty. All that *is* certain is that the lords of the Ring have changed. The earliest lords were Celtic Pagans who mixed their mysterious brews in enormous magic cauldrons placed in the middle of the Ring. There are even rumours that human sacrifice was included in their rituals, with adults, or even children, being added to the cauldron's brew."

This latest revelation increased the Ring's eeriness, my emotions recoiling in horror at the thought of the human sacrifice which may have taken place on the very spot I was standing.

Yore gauged my reaction and responded accordingly.

"I also find it hard to believe that people blessed with living on the soil of Sussex should make human blood sacrifices. But who knows? The past keeps many of its dark secrets to itself. Even those who belong to the past, such as I, are not granted with the vision to see its darkest parts."

"So you don't know everything then?" Yo! jibed irreverently.

"No," Yore replied solemnly, "I only have vision to see the Light, thank God. The ways of Darkness are concealed from me."

"Go on," I urged, enthralled by the tale Yore was weaving.

"After many centuries the gods of the Celts were replaced by new unhappy lords from the East. The Romans brought with them to England the worship of the Persian god, Mithras, and it was the lords of Mithras who inherited the Ring. A temple to the Persian god was built here and the cult was practised on this site for three hundred years. It was not until St Wilfrid, St Cuthman and other followers of the True God had driven the old gods away that the Ring ceased to be a Pagan place. But then perhaps it is still a Pagan place. A Pagan place asleep. It is said that anyone who runs round the Ring seven times without stopping will raise the Devil from out of the centre of it. Satan will then offer him a magic drink from a goblet of gold. It is the cup of damnation."

Yore's words died away ominously and an eerie hush followed.

"This is too much!" Yo! exclaimed, shattering the silence. "What complete and utter drivel!"

Yore smiled. "Possibly," he conceded.

"I shall prove that it is drivel," said Yo! defiantly.

"How?" I asked.

"By conducting a little scientific experiment."

"This should be interesting," Yore chuckled.

"I now propose to run round the Ring seven times without stopping."

"That's a little risky, don't you think?" said Yore, trying hard to smother a smirk.

"It is not in the least risky. As the Devil doesn't exist,

he is hardly likely to appear is he?"

"But what if he does exist?"

"He doesn't."

"Then what is the point of conducting the experiment?"

"To prove to you that he doesn't exist."

Without further ado, Yo! began to run briskly around the circumference of the Ring. Once. Twice. Three times.

"I think we had better vacate the centre of the Ring," Yore suggested after Yo! had completed his fourth lap.

"Why?" I asked. "You don't really believe that anything is going to happen, do you?"

"It is better to be safe than sorry," Yore insisted.

We walked towards the perimeter as Yo! completed lap five.

From the safety of the Ring's edge, I watched as Yo! started his final lap. It was certainly a strange setting for a mad experiment and I found myself both troubled and tickled by a macabre mirth. I didn't know whether to laugh or fly. Altogether an unsettling sensation.

At last Yo! completed his last circuit. As he did so we all stood staring expectantly at the centre of the Ring. It was a totally irrational act because I don't believe any of us expected anything to happen, not even Yore. All was silent except for Yo!'s exhausted breathing. We were right. Nothing happened. Wait. We were wrong. Something was happening. Something really strange. As we watched, the centre of the circle began to subside slowly. Then the subsidence gained momentum. Soon there was a landslide towards the centre, leaving an abyss before us. A seemingly bottomless pit, filled with unfathomable darkness.

"Oh my God!" I shrilled in terror.

"I doubt it," said Yore.

Yo! gaped agog, lost for words.

Finally, out of the darkness emerged a huge, hideously grotesque figure, reddish violet in colour.

"It's . . . it's . . . him!" I spluttered, hoping he would

not offer me a drink from his golden goblet.

Suddenly there was a change. The figure turned an electric blue and floated out of the pit.

I laughed hysterically, more relieved than I had ever been in my life. It was not the Devil at all, but Yet emerging from one of his claret sleeps. He drifted away from us aimlessly, humming Yardish expletives contentedly to himself.

A veritable volcano of chalk and earth filled the pit from which he had risen so that all was as it had been before Yo!'s experiment.

"Yo! Yet!" shouted Yo!, his own relief clearly apparent.

"Yards! Yo!" shouted Yet as he drifted northwards. "Mega-yards-powerpl... Avant-garde!"

The electric blue humanoid balloon suddenly found itself caught up in the branches of one of the beech trees encircling the Ring.

"Magpie!" shouted Yet, tree-trapped.

"Yo!" exlaimed Yo!, amused at the sight.

Yet hung helplessly, struggling vainly to disentangle himself.

"Well," Yore chuckled, "in all my days I have never seen an elephant up a tree."

"Or a beeched whale," I added.

"Beeched whale!" laughed Yore. "Very good!"

"Get me down!" Yet demanded.

"You often do," said Yore.

"Help! Mega-avant-garde-powerplay-in-earnest! Magpie!"

"Ah," said Yore, clearly enjoying the moment, "if you were a magpie you could get down easily."

"Megamag!"

"One of us had better help him," I said.

"Not I," said Yore, smiling. "When it comes to the tree of life I deal with the roots, not the branches."

"And I'm not getting these designer jeans dirty," Yo!

insisted.

"I suppose that leaves me," I said resignedly.

"Leaves you," Yore laughed. "Very good!"

"Is it?" I replied irritably, making my way to the foot of the large beech tree.

"Yards," said Yet hopefully as I began to climb.

"Avant," I muttered.

Eventually I succeeded in clambering onto the branch which held Yet captive. With difficulty I disentangled the blue whale and his flabby, flacid flesh flopped to the ground, bouncing on impact.

"Yards!" he exclaimed, floating back into an upright position.

Slowly I climbed back down and rejoined the motley crew.

"Yo!" said Yo! "What's happening Yet!"

"Nothing's happening yet," said Yore.

"Lapwinging," said Yet.

"What?" said Yo!

"Lapwinging!"

"What's lapwinging?"

"Lapwinging is mega-yards-powerplay!"

"Sounds good!" said Yo!

"Yards!" said Yet, holding out his hand to Yo!. "Let's lapwing!"

Yo! grabbed Yet's outstretched hand and was whisked away heavenwards, over the Ring and out of sight.

"What's lapwinging?" I asked Yore, repeating Yo!'s question.

Yore shrugged dismissively.

"If it doesn't involve keeping one's feet on the ground I'm not interested," he said.

Walking slowly, we continued our journey. Leaving the Ring, we also left the South Downs Way, taking a steep bridlepath downhill through woodland.

"Trees," said Yore as we descended deciduously. "We shall pay homage to the trees."

I had never paid homage to trees before but in the gloaming of their gloom I felt a mysterious aura which made Yore's words singularly appropriate.

"Unlike trees," he continued, "we only have our feet *on* the ground. They have their feet *in* the ground, in joyous communion with the soil of Sussex. And," he added, "they are not only rooted in space but in time also. The mighty oak lives for countless generations of men, observing the changes and keeping the secrets of history."

Yore fell silent for a moment as though in contemplation. The only sound as we passed through the twilit trees was birdsong and the snapping of dead wood under foot. Presently my companion continued.

"Once there were many more trees than there are now. Most of Sussex was peopled by trees and the trees far outnumbered the people. Sussex was one large sacred forest. The Great South Wood. Even London was a forest. Norwood was the Great North Wood which stretched from Croydon right up to Forest Hill. In those days Croydon and London were connected by a canal which passed through the forest, and so dense were the trees that it was said that the sun never reached the waters of the canal. The soil of the Great North Wood was clay, most suitable for large majestic oaks, only a few of which still survive. The vast majority were not so fortunate, being smothered by the suburban sprawl as it crawled southward."

Having paid homage, Yore fell into a wistful silence.

We left the woods and followed a footpath across open country to the village of Washington. Arriving at the Frankland Arms I assumed that we would stop for refreshment but Yore stopped me as I made to cross the threshold.

"No," he said, "this inn is too enshrined in the past to be blasphemed by the present. The Frankland Arms is a shrine to what is lost. The Michell's ale sold here was the best in the whole of God's creation but, alas, the ale is no more. The inn without the ale is like a church without the

Blessed Sacrament. It is an empty tomb. We will not enter."

Disappointed, I followed him as we strode away from the inn, past the church and across a dual carriageway. Yore passed over the A24 in mournful silence and would not speak again until we had climbed to the top of Barnsfarm Hill and were once more on the roof of the Downs.

We continued westward and Yore informed me that the town of Storrington lay at the foot of the hill. I took his words on faith because the town was invisible in the murky depths of the morning. We surmounted Sullington Hill, Chantry Hill and Kithurst Hill and so journeyed on. As we did so, visibility deteriorated further and I felt a sense of frustration at my inability to enjoy the views Yore described to me. I was as a blind man being told of the beauties he could never see.

Slowly the frustration passed and was replaced by a romantic realisation that the murkiness bestowed a beauty of its own on the wildness of the Downs. Mistery. All around the undulating curves faded into barely distinguishable shades of grey. The Sussex landscape became a wonderful incarnation of a Turner seascape. A masterpiece in monochrome.

With this more positive outlook I listened eagerly as Yore pointed in the direction of Parham House, an Elizabethan mansion, which lay, apparently, a mile to the north in a beautiful deer park, invisible but inviolate.

We climbed Rackham Hill and soon began to descend towards the Vale of Arun. Yore's spirits seemed to lift visibly. And so did the drizzly mist, opening a vista of wealden wilderness before us. All became bright and clear, as though a veil had been lifted from our eyes.

"Arun!" Yore exclaimed, drinking drunkenly great draughts of the view. "I can almost taste her waters from here!"

I didn't know the river and had no store of nostalgia with which to savour the view but, be that as it may, it was beautiful beyond description. The overall impression, as we looked down on the river, snaking its way through mile upon mile of unspoilt countryside, was one of sparseness. An empyrean emptiness. Man was still a stranger here. He didn't belong in such an Eden. Certainly *I* felt like a stranger. A stranger in a strange country. A stranger in paradise. I felt as though I should tread softly in case I disturbed the dream.

"This is no dream," Yore said, interjecting my thoughts. "Reality is more beautiful than any dream."

At that moment I found his statement all too easy to believe.

We walked on a little further in entranced silence until Yore broke the spell with a bisyllabic exclamation.

"Dragons! We can't spend St George's Day in Sussex without discussing dragons. Sussex dragons! Especially as the most famous dragon of all lived in this valley."

"Dragons?" I replied, grinning. "It seems hard to believe that anything as nasty as a dragon could live in a place as beautiful as this."

"Ah, but didn't the serpent manage to worm his way into Eden?"

"Allegedly," I said.

"Allegorically," Yore retorted.

"Either way," he continued, "I must tell you of the fearsome dragon of Arun."

"Go on," I laughed, resigned to another tale of Yore.

"The dragon was not a common dragon for, as you know, common dragons are land-dwelling beasts. The dragon of Arun was a water monster who lived in the knucker hole, a large pool continuously freshened by underground springs. A very desirable residence for a dragon of the aquatic variety."

I laughed. "A des res for dragons!"

"Any way, the dragon would emerge from the hole whenever he was hungry with only one thing on his mind. Food. And you know, of course, that dragons are notoriously fussy eaters."

"I didn't actually," I confessed.

"Well, any self-respecting dragon will only eat one type of food. A fair damsel."

"Of course," I sniggered, "why didn't I remember? How silly of me."

"This particular dragon had a voracious apetite so that, very soon, there was a distinct shortage of fair damsels in the whole Vale of Arun. A very distinct shortage. In fact, in the end, there was only one fair damsel left. The king's daughter."

"Really?" I gasped, feigning surprise.

"And the king, naturally enough, didn't want his daughter to be eaten."

"No, and I don't suppose she was struck on the idea either!"

"Quite. Well, the king kept the princess locked up in Arundel castle so that the dragon couldn't get his claws on her."

"Or his teeth."

"In the end, of course, the dragon became *very* hungry. And you know what happens when a dragon becomes very hungry?"

"He starves."

"No. When a dragon becomes very hungry he becomes *very* angry. He roared all day long and laid siege to the castle, killing anyone who tried to get in or out."

"And spitting them out afterwards obviously, as they weren't fair damsels."

"Obviously. And you know what happened next?"

"No."

"The people in the castle also became very hungry because nobody could get any supplies past the furious dragon."

"A bit of a tricky situation."

"Precisely. Finding himself in this tricky situation the king had to do something. What do you think he did next?"

"It's obvious really. He fed his daughter to the dragon."

"No he did not! The king announced that anybody who slayed the dragon would receive his daughter's hand in marriage."

"Now that's a new twist. I would never have guessed."

"And do you know what happened next?"

"Oh, let me guess, a brave young knight came along, slew the beast, married the princess and they all lived happily ever after."

"How did you know that? Has someone told you the story of the dragon of Arun before?"

"No," I laughed, "not exactly."

"And speaking of dragons . . ." Yore said, pointing to a bizarre sight about a hundred yards ahead in the sky.

I looked in the direction Yore was indicating and saw a large electric blue mass, somersaulting and nosediving wildly, with a designer-clad person hanging onto its arm. They would swoop swiftly, getting treacherously close to the ground before pulling out of the dive at the last moment and rocketing skywards again.

"P'wit, p'wit. Pee-wit! Peeee-wit!" They shouted in unison with every dive, twist or loop-the-loop.

"What a crazy pair!" I exclaimed, laughing at their antics.

"Quite," said Yore.

"What on earth are they doing?"

"Something meaningless, no doubt."

"P'wit, p'wit. Pee-wit! Peeee-wit!" They screamed again as another crash dive aborted at the last moment in a series of acrobatic whirls.

"Why," I said as we got closer, "they're chasing those birds."

"Those birds," said Yore, "are lapwings. And, don't worry, they are oblivious of the presence of the two clowns and are not frightened by their fooling."

"Lapwinging!" I exclaimed. "They're lapwinging! So

that's what it is!"

Lapwinging appeared to involve following lapwings in flight and attempting to mirror their acrobatic, swooping flight patterns and, it seemed, as another "p'wit, p'wit. Pee-wit! Peeee-wit!" disturbed the peace, their distinctive cry.

"Yo!" cried Yo! as he noticed our arrival. "Yooooooooooo!" he screamed again wildly as Yet ascended swiftly.

"P'wit, p'wit. Pee-wit! Peeee-wit!" They both yelled in unison as another perilous, twisting, swirling dive catapulted earthwards. A roller-coaster in thin air. Pulling out of the dive at the last moment, Yet landed safely a few yards in front of us.

"Yaaaards!" he exclaimed wildly, putting Yo! down as he did so.

"Yards!" I replied, laughing at their lunacy.

"What's happening!" Yo! yelled, more as an exclamation than a question.

"We were discussing dragons," I replied chirpily.

"Wicked!" said Yo!

"Invariably," said Yore.

"Wasn't Puff the Magic Dragon a good dragon?" I asked, questioning Yore's assertion and remembering one of my favourite childhood songs.

"There is no such thing as a good dragon," Yore insisted. "Puff, whoever he is, must be a make-believe dragon. Real dragons are always evil."

"Real dragons are always mythical," Yo! countered.

"Rubbish! Real dragons are legendary, they are not mythical."

"What's the difference?" I asked.

"Yo!" said Yo!.

"There is all the difference in the world," Yore asserted solemnly. "Legends and myths are not only different, they are opposites."

"How?" I asked doubtfully.

"Because a myth is a lie and a legend is the truth."

"Nonsense," said Yo!.

"No, nonsense is something else altogether. A legend is not nonsense, nor is it a myth. It is a mystery."

"Hocus pocus!" said Yo! dismissively.

"Precisely," said Yore, "*that* is the greatest mystery of all, although I must say that your Latin is awful."

"This is ridiculous," Yo! complained.

"And it's getting us nowhere," I added.

"On the contrary," said Yore, "it's getting us to the truth. There is a lot of truth to be found in legends."

"What is truth?" Yo! scoffed. "It is undiscoverable."

"It is discoverable in legends."

"Truth is a legend," Yo! countered.

"Thank God for small mercies," Yore smiled, "at least we can agree that it is not a myth!"

Yo! raised his arms in exasperation.

"Yards!" said Yet.

"Take dragons for instance," Yore continued.

"Must we?" I asked, growing weary of the subject.

"Dragons are the best example of the truth of legends," Yore proceeded, ignoring my protest. "All over the world there are stories of dragons. Different cultures which never came into contact with each other all had their own dragon legends. This is too much of a coincidence to be an accident. No, dragons existed, or exist, because they express a truth common to all mankind."

"Which is?" I asked.

"Which is the objective existence of evil."

"Nonsense," Yo! objected.

"Avant-garde," muttered Yet.

"Dragons were the embodiment of evil. They were capable of consuming the weak or foolish, were avoided by the wise and were slain by the good."

"It is time," said Yo!, "for people to throw of these stupid superstitions. We have spent far too long being chased by the dragons of the past."

"It is better to be chased by dragons than to chase

them."

"Chasing the dragon," muttered Yet weakly, his chameleon coat changing colour as he spoke, "that's a yards game."

"Yo!" said Yo!.

"The trouble with chasing the dragon," said Yore solemnly, "is that the dragon always ends up chasing you."

"Avant-garde," moaned Yet, his colour now chameleonised to claret. Slowly he sank.

"Megamag," he mumbled, disappearing beneath the surface of Amberley Mount, "lapwinging always uses the button's magic too quickly."

"He's in good company," Yore smiled, pointing to two tumuli at the side of the path, "those wise old ancient chieftans, resting in peace beneath the soil of their native land, will be able to tell Future about the foolishness of chasing dragons."

"The Future will never be fooled by the Past," said Yo!.

"Then, my dear Present, the Future will only be fooling himself."

The three of us then proceeded downhill, skirting the northern edges of Downs Farms, while Yore continued his monologue on Sussex dragons. He informed us that a dragon had been sighted in Sussex as recently as the seventeenth century. It was seen in the area of St Leonard's Forest and Faygate Forest by four independent witnesses who described the beast as being lizard-shaped, about nine feet long, covered with black scales and with a powerful tail. At the sound of man or cattle it raised its serpentine neck, which was nearly four feet long, and looked around with great arrogance. The sightings were recorded for posterity by a certain John Trundle who travelled from London to investigate the truth or otherwise of the story. He became convinced that the sightings were genuine and published his findings in a pamphlet in 1614.

"So," Yore concluded triumphantly, "dragons may not

only be true, they may be facts also!"

"If that's so," I asked sceptically, "why have none been spotted since?"

"Yo!" said Yo! in agreement.

"Perhaps they have become extinct," Yore replied. "Don't forget that up until a few hundred years ago most of Sussex was dense forest, much of which was uncharted. All sorts of creatures may have lived in them before they were felled in the name of progress."

"Surely not dragons!" I protested.

"Why not?"

"Wouldn't archaeologists have discovered their bones or something?"

"Yo!" said Yo!, urging me on.

"The fact that scientists haven't discovered dragon bones leaves two possibilities," Yore replied. "Either dragons never existed or, which is at least as likely, scientists still haven't discovered their bones! The fallibility of science lies in the fact that it always seeks to paint a final picture when it only has fragments of it. The facts discovered by science so far only form a part of the jigsaw of reality. The overall picture painted by science is a work of art. The art of calculated guesswork. They have to continually re-paint the picture whenever new pieces of the jigsaw are discovered. Science is good when it is science, it is bad when it deludes itself of its omniscience."

"Heavy!" I exclaimed, trying to take it in.

We had now arrived beside a railway line and the distant rumbling heralded the imminent arrival of a train.

"All I can say," said Yo!, "is that dragons are a drag! Catch yer later!"

With that he sprang gazelle-like up the side of the embankment and leapt, leopard-like, onto the roof of the speeding train.

"Yooooooo!!" he waved as he rocketed south.

I waved after him, amazed at his superhuman athleticism, until, within seconds, he had sped out of sight.

By comparison, the progress of Yore and I as we continued on foot was positively snail-like.

"Ah," said Yore, hearing my thoughts, "but we are going in the right direction. Present, typically, is going fast but is going completely in the wrong direction!"

The right direction took us under the railway bridge at Amberley Station and then immediately off the road and onto a footpath running alongside the eastern bank of the River Arun. If anything, Yore seemed even more at peace walking through the lush meadows which embraced the gently flowing river than he had been on top of the wild Downs.

"Allow me," he said, after we had crossed a footbridge to the western bank of the river, "to tell you one more story about Sussex dragons."

I groaned.

"Only one more," he added apologetically. "It is my favourite of all the dragon stories, not least because it concerns that part of Sussex closest my heart."

"Go on," I grinned.

"Well, this is St George's Day and we all know about St George and the Dragon. But few know the story of St Leonard and the Dragon."

"True," I agreed, having heard of neither saint nor dragon.

"The dragon was a large, fearsome creature which prowled through the dense woodland of St Leonard's Forest. Of course, it wasn't called St Leonard's Forest in those days, it was named after the saint in honour of the great deed I am about to recount."

"Carry on," I laughed, wondering how many tangential diversions I would have to endure before his tale was complete.

"Any way, the dragon wandered around looking for its prey and, as time went by, its prowling took it closer and closer to the town of Horsham. The townsfolk were obviously concerned and prayed allowed for God to send them assistance. St Leonard heard their prayers and came to Sussex. He searched the forest and eventually came upon the fearsome dragon. A terrible struggle ensued and the saint slew the beast. But he lost a lot of blood in the battle and, legend has it, wherever a drop of his blood fell, Our Lady's Tears sprang up. Even today, Our Lady's Tears still grow wild in St Leonard's Forest as a permanent reminder of the saint's heroic deed."

"Our Lady's Tears?" I asked, puzzled. "I've never heard of those."

Yore looked wistfully at me.

"You know the flower," he sighed, "but the name is unknown to you. You know it as lily-of-the-valley, but, in a more poetic age before the people of England lost their love for the Mother of God, they were always known as Our Lady's Tears. Sadly, other flowers have also lost their earlier romantic names. Bluebells were once called Mary's Bells, or maribells for short, and marigolds were originally named Mary's Gold."

As Yore concluded his oral and floral tribute to the Virgin, we found our way blocked by dozens of grazing cows. Although we were evidently the cause of great curiosity, with the bovine beasts queueing up for a better view of us, they showed no inclination to move out of our way.

"Moooove!" my colleague demanded, mimicking the beasts.

Their response was one of dumb defiance. Standing dozens deep between us and the stile we needed to traverse, they chewed the cud indifferently. An obdurate obstacle to our further progress.

"Moooove!" Yore repeated.

More stubborn insubordination.

"I warn you," Yore continued, "if you don't move I shall have no option but to use my secret weapon."

The animals were not cowed by the threat. In response there was the odd moo but no movement.

"You've had your chance," Yore continued in mock solemnity. "You give me no choice. I shall have to inflict a sonnet upon you."

"A sonnet!" I laughed. "You're not proposing to recite poetry to the cows are you?"

"I know it is a little cruel," Yore confessed apologetically, "but it's the only way."

I shook my head in disbelief. Meanwhile, the cows were unmoved in both senses of the word, regarding the madman through sad brown eyes.

The madman cleared his throat.

"Lift up your hearts in Gumber, laugh the Weald," he began in deadly earnest, his bemused audience mooing in accompaniment.

"And you my mother the Valley of Arun sing.
Here am I homeward from my wandering,
Here am I homeward and my heart is healed.
You my companions whom the World has tired
Come out to greet me. I have found a face
More beautiful than Gardens; more desired
Than boys in exile love their native place.
Lift up your hearts in Gumber, laugh the Weald
And you most ancient Valley of Arun sing.
Here am I homeward from my wandering,
Here am I homeward and my heart is healed.
If I was thirsty, I have heard a spring.
If I was dusty, I have found a field."

Unbelievably, as Yore concluded the final line of his verse, the cows lumbered nonchalantly out of our path.

"Works every time," muttered my companion as he walked between the beasts and climbed the stile. Flabergasted, I followed him northwards along the banks of the Arun. The weather had improved beyond all expectation and I was happy to bask in the peace of the valley.

Presently we arrived at the village of Bury, nestling on the banks of the river, where we were greeted by the shrill sound of children at play. Although the noise was coming from inside a walled garden so that the children could not be seen, Yore seemed visibly cheered by the invisible source of the joyful music.

"That's more like it!" he said, savouring the moment and grinning broadly. "The noise of festivity as befits a Holy Day!"

"Once," he continued, "every village in England would be filled with the sound of merriment on St George's Day. Everywhere there would be singing and dancing. Morris men and mystery plays!"

As we walked past the church in the sleepy village, I found it easy to imagine the festivities of yore and ghosts of past revellers seemed to dance through the empty streets. Thus comparing the imagined past with the visible present I found myself sharing my companion's wistful regret that the days of festival had passed away.

Continuing our journey through the village, and passing the house where the novelist John Galsworthy had lived, we arrived at the White Horse where, to my great relief, Yore suggested we stop for refreshment.

Our stay was short. A stilton sandwich and a solitary pint of Arundel E.S.B. and we were again on our way. It seemed that Yore only had one objective on his mind. The Cricketers at Duncton which still lay several miles ahead. Having no objection to his objective I kept up with the increased pace he set. We passed through the hamlet of West Burton, past the extensive remains of a Roman villa at Bignor and thence, via a fast-flowing stream through a delightful wood, to Sutton where my eyes looked longingly at the village inn. The desire for a pint of the Young's bitter, tantalisingly advertised in the inn's window, was to remain unsatisfied. Yore would not rest until we reached our final destination.

We crossed several more fields before arriving at the hamlet of Barlavington where we sought brief sanctuary in the tiny church of St Mary's. Resting in its gloomy interior I felt the truth of the adage that small is beautiful. This was one of the most charming churches I had ever visited. Its decor, which included a bas-relief of the Annunciation and stained glass windows behind the altar depicting the Crucifixion and Resurrection, carved a lasting niche in my memory.

Refreshed in spirit, though still in need of the material comforts that the Cricketers promised, we continued the last two miles of our day's journey. Stopping briefly to admire the stately elegance of Duncton Mill, we finally arrived at the Inn of Desire. Crossing the threshold I could see instantly why my colleague had always intended this to be the day's destination. Logs crackled in a blazing fireplace, bathing us in a blanket of welcoming warmth, and exposed beams announced the inn's fifteenth century credentials. The interior was decorated tastefully, as the name of the inn would suggest, with ancient trophies, prints and memorabilia connected with the noble game of cricket.

We sat down at a large wooden table and I ordered two pints of ale.

Yore's countenance was one of utter contentment as he beamed across the table at me.

"It is good to be back! It's been a long, long time. Many, many years. But the place has worn well."

"I have never been here before," I answered, "but it's a good pub."

"Ah!" Yore sighed, leaning back in his chair, "listen to that music!"

I was puzzled. There was no music.

"Precisely," said Yore, "no music except the sweet tune of convivial conversation."

He was right. The only sound was the hum of human voices, emanating mainly from a group of locals gathered round the bar. I looked around. There were no machines of any description. No flashing fruit machines. No juke box. Nothing.

"As an inn should be!" Yore exclaimed, hearing my thoughts and observing my observations.

I smiled. "I'm not so sure Yo! would agree!"

Yore returned my smile with a broad grin of his own. "No," he replied.

"Nor would he go much on the menu," I laughed. "No burgers!"

I ordered deepfried brie with redcurrant jelly for both of us as a starter and partridge in cognac for myself as a main course. Yore selected the duck breast with honey and brandy and, of course, the compulsory bottle of Burgundy. As we waited for our food to arrive, I again studied the inn's interior. It was certainly a monument to cricket with every wall adorned with mementos of one sort or another.

"The inn is a shrine, a secular shrine, to James Dean," Yore remarked.

"Surely not!" I replied in disbelief.

"Why not?" Yore asked.

"Well," I replied, still puzzled, "why would James Dean come to a place like this?"

"Why wouldn't he?" Yore retorted scornfully.

"I wouldn't have thought it was his scene," I replied. "I can't really see James Dean drinking a pint at the Cricketers!"

"*He* often drank at the Cricketers!" Yore insisted.

"I didn't know that he ever came to England," I said.

"What on earth are you talking about?" Yore remonstrated.

"James Dean."

"The cricketer."

"The film star."

"Who?"

"James Dean the film star."

"Never heard of him," Yore replied dismissively. "I'm talking of the *famous* James Dean. The Sussex cricketer who invented over-arm bowling."

"Oh," I said, enlightened but still confused.

"He once lived at this inn and he used to walk all the way from Duncton to Brighton to play cricket for Sussex."

Our *hors-d'oeuvres* arrived. Substantial wedges of brie coated in breadcrumbs. Yore muttered grace to himself in Latin and then we both tucked in with relish, the crispness of the breaded coat contrasting succulently with the warm melted interior. Delicious.

"And," Yore continued, finishing a mouthful of cheese, "that is not the only famous cricketing link with this inn."

I looked up from my eating by way of inviting him to continue.

"John Wisden, who founded the famous cricketing almanac, owned the Cricketers at one time."

Sipping my wine, I raised my eyebrows, feigning interest. The truth was that I wasn't particularly interested in cricket.

Yore smiled sympathetically. "To tell the truth," he said, "I'm not a great cricket lover either. During my worldly life, my main sporting pursuit was sailing. I loved the taste of the salt in the air, and the feel of the wind in the sails, and the sight and the power of the wide, wild sea."

He sank back in his chair, eyes distant, in obvious reminiscence of his former life. Presently, reaching for the wine bottle and replenishing his glass and mine, he returned to the present.

As time elapsed a mood of merriment enlivened the evening. Our respective main courses, accompanied in each case by french beans, courgettes and carrots, went down as satisfactorily as the wine. The meal over, we ordered a second bottle of Burgundy and soaked up the friendly atmosphere.

Discovering that there was no room at the inn I enquired about local bed and breakfast establishments. I was handed a brochure which Yore regarded disdainfully.

"How vulgar," he complained, handing the brochure back to me, "a helevision in every room!"

A moment's silence ensued and the voiceless vacuum enabled us to hear the conversation of the locals at the bar.

THE THREE YS MEN

They were discussing a funeral that had taken place earlier in the day of a local man who had lived in the village all his life. One of the men at the bar was speaking with reverence of the poem which was read as the coffin was lowered. The landlord said he had a copy of it and went to find it. Returning a few moments later, book in hand, the whole place fell silent as the verse was recited.

> He does not die that can bequeath
> Some influence to the land he knows,
> Or dares, persistent, interwreath
> Love permanent with the wild hedgerows;
> He does not die, but still remains
> Substantiate with his darling plains.
> The spring's superb adventure calls
> His dust athwart the woods to flame;
> His boundary river's secret falls
> Perpetuate and repeat his name,
> He rides his loud October's sky:
> He does not die. He does not die.
> The beeches know the accustomed head
> Which loved them, and a peopled air
> Beneath their benediction spread
> Comforts the silence everywhere;
> For native ghosts return and these
> Perfect the mystery in the trees.
> So, therefore, though myself be crosst
> The shuddering of that dreadful day
> When friend and fire and home are lost
> And even children drawn away -
> The passer-by shall hear me still,
> A boy that sings on Duncton Hill.

A momentary hush followed the recital before a gentle chorus of approval filled the inn. I looked across at Yore and was surprised to see him weeping. My eyes met his questioningly but his, tear-filled, were unable to answer.

"Do you know that poem?" I asked.

"Yes, very well," he sighed. "I wrote it."

My eyes widened in astonishment but I said nothing. We fell into a mellow and melancholy silence. I alone with my thoughts and Yore alone with his memories.

Eventually it was Yore who spoke.

"It's strange to hear future generations repeating words written all those years ago. Very strange."

Shaking his head slowly, he continued.

"The body decays but the spirit remains and fame outlives the flesh. *Dominum non dignum est.* I am not worthy."

Finally he mumbled in a muffled, hoarse whisper:

"He does not die that can bequeath
Some influence to the land he knows . . .
He does not die. He does not die."

The Twenty-fourth of April, 1996

The morning wore a melancholy mask. During the night the words of Yore's poem had repeated themselves insistently in my semi-consciousness, haunting my dreams.

"He does not die. He does not die."

But he *did* die. And so did the local man who had requested the words be recited over his grave yesterday. They were both dead. Yet Yore was alive as well as dead. It was all too much. And what of Yo!? Was he alive or dead? If he was the Ghost of Sussex Present he couldn't be dead. Could he? And as for Yet, surely he hadn't been born? My head ached with the incongruities. Sleep was impossible.

Rising, I switched on the television - or helevision as Yore had dubbed it the previous night. My hope was that real human voices would exorcise the ghosts in my head. No such luck. The voices were real but the words were surreal. Inanity bordering on insanity. I smiled grimly. The inane preaching to the insane!

Was I insane? Was life inane? Or was life insane and my attempts to rationalise it merely inane? Too many questions. No answers.

I switched off the television. If reality existed it wasn't to be found in that particular box. Contemplating Yore's remark, I decided that whether or not the t.v. offered a vision of hell, whatever hell was, it certainly didn't offer a vision of reality. Unless reality *was* insane. I smiled again. The lunatics had taken over the asylum!

By the time I went down for breakfast the melancholy had made way for moroseness. This was accentuated by a sudden and sullen realisation that my days with Yore were almost at an end. Today, so he had informed me yesterday, we would reach the westernmost edge of his county. The consummation of our journey.

It was true that part of me was relieved at the fact. I had grown weary physically by the four days of walking and weary also of the emotional intensity of my ghostly guide. But behind any feelings of relief there lingered a feeling of resentment. I was having an adventure beyond my wildest dreams with creatures beyond the realms of my imagination. More importantly, we had touched on things which seemed to really matter so that the prospect of a return to the office filled me with dread. The suit I would have to don again on Monday suddenly seemed morbid and macabre. The tie was a rope round my neck, and the jacket was a strait jacket. The office itself was the padded cell to which I was condemned, a soft cell specialising in the hard sell.

God help me!

I smiled. Was there a God? Clearly Yore thought so. Equally clearly, Yo! didn't. I didn't know. And what did Yet think of God? *Did* Yet think of God? Did Yet think? Questions. Always questions. And precious few answers.

Finishing breakfast and settling the bill, I walked down to the Cricketers where, as arranged, Yore was waiting for me. He greeted me cheerfully enough, enthusing about the rare nature of the inn sign under which he was standing. Apparently, it was unusual because it was double-sided, commemorating James Dean on one side and W. G. Grace on the other. He pointed to each side to illustrate the depictions of the two cricketers but realised immediately that I was not in a particularly receptive mood.

Thereafter, he seemed happy to mirror my muted mood, leaving me in sullen silence. Wordlessly we walked westward, skirting the northern perimeter of Seaford College, a large public school. It wasn't until we reached Lavington Stud Farm that the serenity of our surroundings lifted my spirits. The sight of two yearlings frolicking friskily and biting each other's head collars brought a smile to my severely solemn features. Further fields revealed mares in foal and mares and foals together. In another field a young girl was lunging a horse and the sight of two deer, startled as we turned a corner, finally purged me of my purgatorial misery. *This* was real and *this* was beautiful!

Leaving the Stud we came across a village school where young children chased each other in an ecstasy of innocence, the human equivalent of the frolicking yearlings. It seemed that the whole world was at play. Yore and I sat outside the church and watched the rush and excitement in the playground. Boys and girls bedecked in red uniforms raced about, each in their own microcosmic world of discovery. The sound of their shrill chorus of purity filled the air and seemed like a babbling brook to my troubled mind. I looked around at the idyll in which I found myself. A tiny school beside a village church, resting in a lush wealden landscape at the foot of afforested downs. An oasis of sanity in a mad world.

The ringing of a handbell signalled the end of playtime for the children and the end of our brief rest. As the children filed back into the classroom, I followed Yore westward. Soon we were climbing steeply through woodland until we had once more reached the roof of the Downs and rejoined the South Downs Way. Travelling the ancient path for a couple of miles we drank in the views across the rolling hills to the south before descending into Cocking for rest and refreshment at the Bluebell inn.

Yore, saddened again to find a busy road ripping through a village he had once known well, would not stay long at the inn. Seeking the sanctuary of the high hills he led me up the side of Cocking Down, refusing to stop until we had reached the summit. Looking back he frowned at the presence in the adjoining field of a tractor which was muckspreading.

"Even in the high places there is no escape from the infernos," he sighed. But the smell of freshly spread muck in his nostrils, and the sight of the wealden panorama prostrate below, cheered him. He smiled contentedly.

"You know," he said, "when all is said and done, Sussex is *still* a beautiful county. This view has not changed much since my time. Sussex is a survivor!"

"Yo!" said Yo!, startling us from behind. "What a

stink! It smells like a sewer here."

"It does *not* smell like a sewer," Yore retorted. "It is the smell of nature nourishing nature."

"Then nature stinks!" Yo! replied, pinching his nose.

No sooner had Yo! made his surprise appearance than the other member of our motley crew emerged from under the newly spread muck.

"Avant-garde!" he exclaimed as the dung clung to his claret garment.

"Phew!" Yo! shouted across to him, "I don't think much of your sleeping arrangements!"

"Magpie!" Yet replied, feebly trying to dislodge the manure.

Yore, laughing heartily, also shouted across to the unfortunate muck-covered figure in the next field.

"I must say," he chuckled, "I never thought the future would look and smell so good and natural!"

"Avant! I'll soon change that!" Yet snapped, pressing a button on his chest. Immediately an oily chemical exuded from pores in his claret covering. Slowly it oozed down his body, removing the muck as it went.

"Yards! That's better!" he exclaimed, pressing the magic button on his wrist, metamorphosing to garish blue and flying across to join us. As he approached, I noticed a sickly, synthetic smell emanating from his person. Evidently the goo he had cleaned himself with.

"Why do farmers still insist on such old-fashioned methods of fertilisation?" he complained, pointing at the muckspreading tractor.

"Because it keeps nature in balance," Yore replied.

"Eco-systems," I added, agreeing with Yore and screwing up my nose at Yet's chemical odour.

"Avant-garde," Yet said. "Eco-systems are megamag!"

"Eco-systems are a fact," I insisted, annoyed at Yet's lack of ecological awareness. At that moment the morning's question returned to me. Did Yet think?

"Do I think?" Yet replied instantly, demonstrating that he had as much ability to read my thoughts as Yore.

"Do I think?" he repeated, obviously aggrieved at the insult.

"I . . . I'm sorry," I said, "I didn't realise you were able to read my thoughts."

"Avant-garde! You should keep your thoughts to yourself!"

"How can I," I said, "when everyone around here gatecrashes them?"

"Then don't think?" Yet snapped.

"I think," said Yore, "that he was wondering whether you do."

"What?" said Yet.

"Think," said Yore.

"Think?" asked Yet.

"Yes, think," Yore repeated. "Cognition. Cogitation. The process of exercising the mind otherwise than by the passive reception of another's ideas. You know, think."

"*You* think," Yet responded, "*I* know."

"Know what?"

"The Future."

"Ah!" Yore sneered. "The Future. The great Unthinkable!"

"It is only unthinkable to you because you are ignorant of its promises."

"If the Future makes promises," Yore countered, "it is certain that it breaks them."

"Avant! The Future is inevitable."

"The Future is a liar!"

"Tomorrow belongs to me!"

"Tomorrow never comes!"

"*I* am Tomorrow!"

"How terribly frustrating for you. Always so close, and yet so far from existence."

"Meaga-avant-garde-powerplayin earnest! Megamag!" Yet snapped, clearly losing all patience with

Yore's ripostes. "You've asked for it. I will tell you the Future and you won't like it at all."

"Science fiction?"

"Science fact!"

"But is it the truth?" Yore jibed, clearly enjoying the verbal duel.

"For God's sake let him speak!" I interjected loudly.

"Yo!" said Yo!.

Yore smiled. "For *His* sake I shall."

Yet, vacillating about two feet off the ground, took a deep breath and began speaking with the gravity his body defied.

"The future is freedom. Freedom from pain. Freedom from suffering. Freedom from superstition. Freedom from religion. Freedom from deformity. Freedom from imperfection."

"Yo!," said Yo!.

Yore hurumphed in an agitated fashion but resisted the temptation to interject.

It was I who spoke next.

"That's all very wonderful and high-sounding but how are all these freedoms to be attained?"

"By controlling nature. By making the planet our slave."

"I'm not sure I like the sound of that," I said. "Our freedom depends upon the planet's slavery?"

"Yards!" Yet affirmed. "In the past we have been slaves of the planet. Our freedom in the future depends upon the planet becoming a slave of us."

"How?" I asked, scratching my head.

"By mastering the eco-systems."

"How?" I asked again.

"By mastering the geno-systems."

"Pardon?"

"The geno-systems."

"The what?"

"Yards!" Yet laughed, obviously amused at my

ignorance. "The answer is in the genes."

"Yo!" said Yo! "I like that. The answer's in the jeans. Skin-tight. Designer. Saville Row. Yo!"

"No Yo!" said Yet. "Not jeans, genes. The genetic revolution."

"Revolution. Yo!"

"Genetic revolution?" I asked. My brow furrowed. Intrigued.

"Yards! The most important revolution in history, only it hasn't happened yet."

"Go on," I urged.

"Well, you've heard of the industrial revolution?"

"Of course."

"And the communications revolution?"

"Yes."

"And the silicon revolution?"

"Computers."

"Yards! But the genetic revolution will be far more important than all of them put together! Or, to put it another way, if computers are yards, genetic engineering is mega-yards-powerplay!"

"Why?"

"Because genetic engineering makes us the masters of everything. We give the orders. Nature obeys."

"I don't understand."

"Avant-garde! Let me explain. You know that many traits are inherited from parent to offspring?"

"Yes."

"Well, for hundreds, maybe thousands, of years we have genetically manipulated organisms to suit our own needs. Pedigrees of dogs have been created by taking offspring in a litter of pups and using those with desirable traits to breed with others exhibiting the same traits. This is known as inbreeding and, as a consequence of selective inbreeding we can slowly remove undesirable genes from a population and the gene pool. Eventually we have individuals of true, pure breeding."

"Finc," I replied, "but how does all this affect us?"

"Because the genetic revolution will make it possible to control the genetic make-up of every organism. Don't you see, in the past the process of pure, selective breeding took many generations because we were reliant on the time it takes for an organism to reach sexual maturity and gestation periods. It took many generations to remove genetic variability and undesirable traits before the pure breeding status was reached. But not in the future."

"Not in the future?"

"No, because the future will gain control of the genosystems. Genetic engineering will allow us to alter genes at will."

"I still don't understand."

"It's all about sequencing DNA. Analysing macromolecules. Codons. Amino acids. The i.d. of genes on chromosomes."

"Hold on, hold on!" I interjected, rubbing my eyes in abject confusion. "This is all too much for me!"

"Yards! Let's just say that the manipulation of genes puts us in total control of the planet and all its resources."

"I'll take your word for it," I said resignedly.

"Yards! But better still it puts us in total control of ourselves."

"How?"

"Because we can become the exact genetic type we want to be. We can be perfect simply by undergoing a course of geno-ops where all undesirable genes are removed."

"Perfect? What's perfect?"

"A human type with no disease, no mental or physical handicaps. No sickness. No need for pain or suffering. A perfect world. Mega-yards-powerplay!"

"Yo!" said Yo!. "Real cool!"

"Yards!" Yet replied, "and that's not all!"

"You mean there's more!" I exclaimed with incredulity.

"Much more! Take sex for instance."
"Sex?"
"Yes, barbaric isn't it? Dirty."
"Is it?"
"Of course, as you are a child of the past, or the present as it appears to you, you are still caught up in the mistaken notion that sex is a desirable thing."
"Isn't it?"
"No, sex is magpie!"
"Sometimes perhaps, but surely not always?"
"Always," Yet insisted.
I shook my head. Lost for words.
Yet sighed patronisingly. "I see you are hopelessly unenlightened. You are a slave to sex and that is the problem."
"Hardly a slave," I protested.
"Yes," Yet insisted, "a slave. You are a slave to your sex-drive. It affects everything you do. The way you behave. The way you respond to others. Your ambition. Your needs. Your wants. Everything. Yes, you are a slave. No doubt about it."
"*I* have a doubt about it."
"Avant-garde! That's because you don't know any better. Future generations will want to be free of the degrading attachment to sex. Overcoming sex is the final frontier. It is the last great barbarity enslaving humankind to nature. Conquest of sex is the final conquest of nature."
I shook my head. Unconvinced.
"And it's so easy!" Yet continued.
"Is it?"
Yet produced a handful of pills from somewhere on his person.
"Yes, all you need is a course of these."
"What are they?"
"Celibo! They're yards! The wonderdrug of the future. So new they haven't been invented yet!"
"Celibo?"

"Mega-yards-powerplay! Celibo! One course of these and your sex-drive is gone forever!"

"No thanks."

"Then there's my favourite," Yet continued, producing a handful of white cubes. "Castro, cube or tablet form. Mega-yards-powerplay-in-earnest!"

"And what do they do?" I asked, dreading the answer but letting my curiosity get the better of me.

"Castro! Mega-yards! Take them for twenty-eight days and your genitalia lose their masculine or feminine characteristics. The final symbolic victory over sexuality! Yards! No more battle of the sexes because there are no more sexes!"

"That's certainly a final solution," I muttered.

"Yards!"

"But," I continued, asking the obvious question, "how do you reproduce."

"We don't."

"You don't reproduce?"

"No."

"But surely the future would soon become extinct?"

"Ah! We don't *re*produce. We produce. Babies are produced to order. The purchaser keys in the required genetic composition of the baby they require and the geno-labs do the rest."

"Yo!" said Yo! "Designer babies!"

"It is a logical progression," Yore said, involving himself for the first time in the bizarre conversation. "The present begets the future."

"I don't understand," I said.

"It's simple really," Yore explained. "Present worships the godgets and Future has become one."

"Yards!" said Yet.

"Yo!" said Yo!, kneeling in a pro-genetic genuflection, "I worship you O Godget!"

"Mega-yards-powerplay!"

"Yo! This calls for a celebration!"

THE THREE YS MEN

Suddenly Yo! had a burger in his hand which he appeared to produce from nowhere.

"Want some?" he asked, holding it in my direction.

"I told you," I replied smiling, "I don't. But how do you do that?"

"What?" said Yo!.

"Produce a burger like that?"

Yo! laughed. "Fast food!" he said.

"Want some?" he continued, this time holding the burger in the direction of Yet.

"I don't," said Yet.

Yo! look deflated and disappointed.

"You don't eat burgers?" he said.

"No, I don't eat," said Yet.

"You don't eat?"

"No."

"You don't eat *anything*?"

"No," Yet replied. "Photosynthetic."

"What?"

"Photosynthetic. I get all the energy I need from the sun. That's what this electric blue skin is for."

For the first time, Yo! looked less than happy with one of Yet's answers. He could accept all Yet's other visions but the prospect of a future without burgers didn't bear thinking about.

"Yards!" said Yet, endeavouring to win his erstwhile ally over.

"Yo!" said Yo! uncertainly.

"Ready for a trip?" Yet continued, understanding Yo!'s weakness.

"Yo!" said Yo! enthusiastically, already forgetting his earlier doubts.

"Yards!" said Yet. "How about some jet-skiing?"

Yo! looked disappointed. "I've done that already. Last week at Brighton."

"Yards!" laughed Yet. "Not *that* jet skiing. Real jet-skiing!"

Yo! looked up with renewed interest. "Real jet-skiing?"

"Yards! Skiing on real jets. That one for instance," he added, pointing to an aeroplane several thousand feet in the air.

"Yo!"

"Yards!"

Yo! grabbed Yet's arm and the two took off vertically, rocket-fashion, and hurtled skyward at phenomenal speed. Within seconds they were a dot in the distance heading towards the jet.

I looked at Yore and laughed.

"If that's the shape of the future give me the present!" I said.

"Or the past," he replied, grinning.

We set off westward again, following the high Downs for a further two miles before Yore stopped.

"We are now at the top of Didling Hill," he said, "and it is here that we must bid our final farewell to the Downs."

I was deeply saddened by the prospect, having grown strangely attached over the last few days to those high, rolling hills.

"You know," I began slowly, "it's weird but I feel as though the Downs are a part of me. Walking in their company for days on end they seem to have seeped into my being, lodging a place in my very soul."

Yore nodded, seeming to sympathise fully with my sentiments.

We were still, staring across the Downs and feeling their undulating embrace. It was Yore who broke the silence by breaking into verse:

> "The great hills of the South Country
> They stand along the sea;
> And it's there walking in the high woods
> That I could wish to be,
> And the men that were boys when I was a boy
> Walking along with me."

Taking a last, long, lingering look at the Downland

roofscape, I followed my companion as he descended into the weald.

At the foot of the hill we came across a tiny, ancient church and a field of new-born lambs. Visions of both the past persistent and the present reborn.

"And the vision is singularly appropriate," said Yore, hearing my thoughts, "for this church, standing alone at the foot of the Downs, has always been known as the Shepherds' Church."

As we walked along the tiny isolated lane between Didling and Treyford, Yore told me how the Shepherd's Church had almost fallen into ruin because of the foolishness of one woman. Apparently, during the mid-nineteenth century, the local Rector appealed to Mrs Vernon Harcourt of West Dean House who owned most of the land thereabouts for money to restore the saxon church of St Paul at Elsted and the Shepherds' Church at Didling. She refused but announced proudly that instead she would erect a great new one between the two at Treyford. The Rector objected but the woman insisted. The great church of St Peter's was built and became known as the "Cathedral of the Downs". It was ill conceived and short-lived because within a hundred years it showed signs of severe structural failure. By then, starved of the much needed funds for repair, the Shepherds' Church was in ruins and the saxon church of St Paul in Elsted was in a similarly poor state. All seemed lost but, as Yore recounted with relish, this was to be another story of resurrection. Life after death. In the middle of this century the Rector of Elsted again launched an appeal for funds, a hundred years after his predecessor's failure. Enough money was raised to repair St Paul's and in 1951 it was rededicated by the Anglican Bishop of Chichester. At the same time the "Cathedral of the Downs" was completely demolished with the aid of explosives.

"A perfect example of pride preceding a fall!" Yore exclaimed, concluding his tale as we arrived at Treyford village.

Yore also informed me that the Shepherds' Church had itself been restored recently so that the whole episode had a happy ending. The ruins of the ill-fated "Cathedral", Yore pointed out, could be seen on the far side of the houses we were now approaching. But my attention was drawn to something unusual on this side of one of the houses. It was a wayside shrine, more reminiscent of Italy than Sussex, depicting St Christopher carrying the Christ child. Underneath were the words:

Who Carried Christ
Speed Thee Today
And Lift Thy Heart Up
All The Way

Whether it was the work of St Christopher or merely my own psychological predispositions I couldn't say, but the dedication achieved its aim. My heart lifted upon the reading of it.

Following footpaths across open country, we wended our way westward. To the east of East Harting we took a steep path through woods to a stream at the bottom. Crossing it, we began to ascend the hill on the other side when the strangest succession of noises caused us to look behind.

Whirrrr! Clank! Clunk! Squeak! Screeeeech! Splash! Squelch! "Damn!"

The last of the noises was clearly discernible as a human voice and looking round we beheld the strangest of sights. There, stuck in the mud in the stream we'd just crossed was an oddly-dressed man on the weirdest of contraptions. The man was young, twenty-something-or-other, sported a long moustache and had well-groomed and greased-back hair which looked the more absurd because of the preposterous position he found himself in. Strangest of all were the clothes the stranger was wearing. Clearly Victorian. As though he had stepped out of a Dickens novel. Equally strange was the apparatus upon which he was perched. It was like a cross between a zimmer frame and an antique exercise bike. The stranger was sitting on the saddle and gripped a lever in each hand. The rest of the contraption appeared a twisted combination of metal, ivory and quartz crystal. But no wheels. An exercise bike with no wheels. It didn't make sense.

And the last observation begged another question. If the antique whatever-it-was had no wheels, how on earth had the stranger managed to carry it down the steep hill through the woods? Looking at the twisted metal-work it looked as though it weighed a ton at least! Whatever it was, it wasn't designed to be portable!

"Damn! Damn! Damn!" The stranger exclaimed, fiddling with bits of the gadget and yanking one of the levers backwards and forwards.

"May we be of any assistance?" Yore asked, approaching the stranger.

The stranger looked up, startled by our presence.

"Oh, it's this damn machine," he grumbled, "it's playing me up again."

"What is it?" I asked.

"This," he said proudly, "is a time machine."

"A time machine!" I hooted. "It's a heap of metal bars with levers attached!"

"It is not," the stranger insisted, apparently stung by my contempt, "it is a time machine."

"Don't I know you from somewhere?" asked Yore, staring at the stranger intently. "Your face is familiar."

The stranger stared at Yore for a few seconds and I felt sure that I recognised recognition in his features. Whether this was so he denied the fact.

"No, I don't think so," he replied nervously. "Now how do I go about getting this thing started again? I wonder if the screws need tightening. You don't happen to have a screwdriver, do you?"

"Not the sort of thing I normally carry around with me I'm afraid," I grinned.

"Or perhaps the crystal rods need oiling. Any oil?"

I shook my head.

"Damn!"

"I know who you are," Yore began in an instant of revelation, "you're We..."

"Well pleased to meet you!" the stranger interjected hurriedly, cutting Yore off before he could finish his sentence and gripping his hand firmly.

Yore looked at the stranger suspiciously.

"You are. Aren't you?" he said.

The stranger shifted uneasily on the saddle.

"What I was during my three-dimensional existence is of no consequence," he said. "In the fourth dimension, my name is Tim."

"Tim?"

"Yes, Tim. The Ghost of Time Uncompleted."

"I see," said Yore as though everything was becoming clear.

"I don't," I said, none the wiser.

Tim smiled.

"Let me elucidate. During my three-dimensional existence I longed for the freedom of the fourth dimension."

"Hold on for a moment," I said, "before you go any further would you please tell me what you mean by the fourth dimension?"

Tim smiled again. "Time of course."

"Okay," I said, concentrating. "Carry on."

"During my previous existence, I wanted the freedom of time."

"We all like a little free time," Yore said, grinning.

"Not free time, freedom of time. I wanted to be able to travel through time as easily as I could travel through space."

"But," I said, puzzled. "That's not possible, is it? I mean, time isn't a solid thing. It's not tangible. You can't touch it. Feel it. It isn't actually there, is it?"

"Of course it's there," Tim insisted. "We can't touch it

physically, but we all experience it actually."

"Actually?"

"Yes, every action requires time."

"I see," I said.

"Indeed," Tim enthused, "existence itself requires time."

"Heresy!" Yore interjected. "Temporal existence requires time, as material existence requires matter. Essential existence requires neither. The essence of existence is eternal. Outside time and space."

"There is nothing outside time and space," Tim insisted. "Eternity doesn't exist."

Yore muttered something under his breath but failed to respond coherently.

Tim seized the initiative.

"Allow me to demonstrate why time is necessary to existence."

"Okay, but *please* keep it simple," I pleaded.

"Of course, it *is* simple. As simple as a cube."

"A cube?"

"Yes. For example, can a cube that does not last for any time at all, have a real existence?"

I closed my eyes, grappling with the concept.

"No," I said, "it can't."

"Good!" Tim exclaimed enthusiastically. "Clearly any real existence must have extension in all four directions. Length, breadth, thickness *and* duration."

"You make a rudimentary and fundamental mistake," Yore said slowly when Tim had finished.

"Which is?"

"Which is that you think like a mechanic and not like a mathematician."

"I'm afraid I don't follow you," said Tim.

"That makes two of us!" I added.

"Then I shall explain. Any mathematician will tell you that there are an infinite number of dimensions, none of which rely upon the existence of time."

"This is too much!" I complained.

"The point is," Tim continued, "that mathematics deals with conceptual theories, whereas existence is a matter of practicalities."

"But what if existence is merely a conceptual theory which the Great Mathematician decided to put into perceptual practice?"

"What on earth are you driving at?" Tim exclaimed.

"Simply this. That if time is merely an extension of matter, as you maintain, it must have been brought into existence at the same time as the other three dimensions. It is an act of creation."

Tim looked at Yore for a moment, shaking his head. Then he smiled.

"You know," he began, "even in our previous existence we never could agree, could we?"

"No, and we couldn't agree to differ either," Yore replied, smiling also.

I looked from one to the other.

"Do you two know each other?"

"We did," Yore replied, "in our worldly existences."

"You were friends?"

"Not exactly. We were enemies."

"Time is the great healer," said Tim.

Yore grinned. "No, Love is the great healer."

"Enough!" I said, determined to nip any further esoteric meanderings in the bud.

"Agreed," said Yore, holding out his hand to Tim. "I offer you an honourable truce. The one I was too hard-hearted to offer you in our worldly lives."

Tim took Yore's hand warmly, shook it firmly and then changed the subject.

"When am I?"

"When?"

"Yes."

"Nineteen ninety-six."

"No!"

"I'm afraid so. When should you be?"

"The past. Way past here. I'm not permitted to go forward in time, only back. Damn it, I'll be in serious trouble if *he* finds out."

"Whose he?" Yore asked, clearly intrigued.

"Mr Christopher."

Yore chuckled. "Christopher? The patron saint of time travellers!"

"No, Mr Christopher, the managing director of Starship Enterprises."

"Is that what he calls himself these days," Yore laughed. "Tell me, how did you meet him?"

"It was strange really," Tim confessed. "When I died, or at least shall I say when I thought I died, I expected nothing really. Literally. I didn't believe anything followed after bodily death. Oblivion awaited me and nothing else."

"But?" urged Yore.

"But to my great surprise I woke up. I'm not sure how or where, or when for that matter. Somewhere on the time-space continuum obviously."

"Obviously," Yore grinned.

"And the first thing I remember was Mr Christopher welcoming me to Starship Enterprises. Then he introduced me to Mr Nicholas who presented me with this time machine, an exact replica of the one I had invented in one of my novels."

"Mr Nicholas?" Yore asked, eyebrows raised.

"Yes."

"What did he look like?"

"Why, do you know him?"

"Not personally, but I think I may know of him. Did he have a beard?"

"Yes, a long white beard. Why?"

"Just wondered," Yore replied, sniggering. "Did he charge you for the time machine?"

"No," said Tim, perplexed at Yore's line of questioning.

"No I didn't think he would. He never does."

"Any way," Tim continued, "Mr Nicholas presented me with the time machine and Mr Christopher told me it was for my services to science fiction during my previous existence."

"Really?" Yore replied, hand over his mouth and chuckling uncontrollably.

"I was honoured obviously. Then Mr Christopher told me that he had a very special task for me. My mission was to find the missing link. I was to use the time machine to travel back through time searching for the link between man and the higher apes."

"Any success?" Yore sniggered.

"Not yet. But I'll keep trying. I know it's out there somewhere."

"I wish I had your faith," Yore croaked, tears of laughter filling his eyes.

"Of course," Tim continued, jerking at one of the levers in frustration, "my task would be made easier if this heap of junk was more reliable. It keeps slipping into forward gear. And now," he moaned, hammering one of the quartz rods with his fist, "I can't get the damn thing to go at all."

"Allow me to help," Yore said.

"How?" Tim replied doubtfully, "you don't know anything about time machines, do you?"

"Nothing at all," Yore conceded, "but I have an idea."

He stepped up to the contraption.

"It's an old trick but it just might work."

Tim and I looked on expectantly. Yore stood quite still, crossed himself and closed his eyes. I couldn't believe it. He was praying!

"Really," Tim complained, "this is no time for fooling arou . ."

Clank! Clunk! Glunk! Whirrrr! And the machine vanished into thin air.

"What did you do?" I asked, gaping in disbelief at the

empty space where Tim and the time machine had been moments before.

Yore grinned impishly. "It was nothing. I just had a quick word with Mr Christopher." Without further ado he began to climb the hill, passing a field of sheep and new-born lambs. As I followed behind I could see his shoulders bouncing up and down, convulsed with laughter. The episode we had just witnessed seemed to have given him more pleasure than any of our previous adventures. For my part this latest instalment in the long sequence of events mystified me more than the rest. It was all bizarre beyond comprehension. Too much.

We walked on through East Harting village, taking a quiet lane north in the direction of Nyewood. Real places. Readily perceived. Situated in real space and time. Perceptions. Easy to accept. I smiled. Seeing is believing!

But I had also seen many things which were unbelievable. The Past. The Present. The Future. Time. Concepts incarnated. Concepts perceived! And, most bizarre of all, the concepts seemed more real than the physical world through which I traversed. Closer to the truth, whatever that meant. So much so that the countryside surrounding me seemed to fade from my consciousness, becoming a shadowland of partly perceived reality through which truth travelled almost as a stranger. And wasn't truth itself a concept?

Too many questions.

All this time Yore had walked beside me, no doubt hearing my thoughts but choosing to leave me alone with them. We had left the Nyewood road some time back, had crossed open farmland, followed a farm track and were now walking through Quebec, a tiny hamlet and a haven of tranquility. The views were wonderful. Literally. Full of wonder. Beautiful. Full of beauty. But wasn't beauty itself a concept? Help! No more questions!

Yore smiled.

"Our journey is near its end."

The end. I didn't want it to end. The journey's end. What *was* the journey's end? Its purpose. There *had* to be a purpose.

Yore smiled again but didn't speak.

Following the lane from Manor Farm to Goose Green, we carried straight on to a footpath across a field. The view was marred by the unsightly presence of overhead power cables supported on landscape-scarring pylons. Passing under these we reached a ditch at the far end of the field.

Yore put his arm gently but firmly on my shoulder.

"This is it. The journey's end. Beyond is No Man's Land. We must part."

I was surprised to find tears welling up in my eyes and a choking sensation in my throat. I couldn't speak and, besides, I didn't know what to say.

Suddenly there was a blinding flash of light. Shocking my senses. And again. Lightning and the crackle of electricity.

I looked up and laughed.

In the distance, running along the power lines, was a large electric blue whale carrying a human figure on its shoulders.

"Yet and Yo!!" I exclaimed.

Whenever the blue figure made contact with the power cables a flash of lightning lit the evening sky, a crackle of electricity burst through the air, and both figures blazed with electrified luminosity.

"Yet and Yo!!" I repeated as they reached the pylon under which we stood.

"Yo!"

"Yards!"

With a final flash and crackle, Yet leapt from the power cable and settled in his customary floating position about ten yards in front of us. Dazzling darts of electricity danced on the surface of his body, fizzing frantically. Putting Yo! down, an electrical dart passed between their fingers in a comic copy of Michelangelo's *Creation of Adam*.

THE THREE YS MEN

"Hardly," Yore smiled, reading my observation, "the future can never create the past!"

"Yo!" exclaimed Yo!, as the electrical embers fizzled around his body, "now that's what I call a buzz!"

"Yards!" said Yet.

"You've come to say goodbye, I suppose," said Yore.

"Goodbye?" said Yet. "Avant-garde! I hate goodbyes. I never have to say goodbye. The future is always arriving. I only ever say hello."

"Yo!"

"Then hello," I laughed, holding out my hand to the floating whale.

"Yards!" said Yet, taking my hand.

I pulled away in shock, stung by an electric charge.

"Static," Yet explained.

"Ecstatic!" exclaimed Yo!

"And as for you Yo!" I began, "have you come to say goodbye or hello?"

To my surprise, Yo! burst into song:

"You say goodbye
and I say hello,
Hello, hello,
I don't know why you say goodbye
I say hello,
Hello, hello,
I don't know why you say goodbye
I say hello."

"Inane," muttered Yore.

"The Beatles!" I exclaimed.

"Yo!" said Yo!.

"Hello Goodbye."

"Yo! You got it!" Yo! exclaimed, congratulating me on my musical knowledge.

"Somewhat appropriate," I continued, "because whether you say hello or goodbye, this is still farewell."

I stepped forward and held out my hand to Yo!.

"I guess this is hello, goodbye," I said, grinning sadly.

"Yo! No!" Yo! protested, "The present is always present. I'm always with you. There's no need for goodbyes."

"Avant-garde!" Yet interjected. "You forget that the present always becomes the future."

"Heresy!" Yore countered. "The present always becomes the past."

"Magpie! Your time is up old man."

"Yo! Yore time is up. I like it! Wicked!"

"There is no rest for the wicked," said Yore, "but I hope to earn forgiveness so that I may eventually rest. That is why I am here. To earn forgiveness."

At last, I thought, an answer to a question! An answer which begged more questions perhaps, but an answer none the less. I decided to seek more answers while I still had the chance. Time, for me at least, was beginning to run out.

"Why are you here Yo!?" I asked.

"Yo! I am here because I have no choice. I am always here. The present is ever present!"

"And you Yet? Why are you here?"

Yet smiled.

"I am here," he said, "to bury the past."

Yore looked angry.

"The man who buries the past buries himself. The present needs the past because the past is his memory. If the present forgets the past he becomes like a man with amnesia. He doesn't know who he is, why he is or where he is."

Yet sneered. "It is not where someone is that matters, still less is it where he has been. What matters is where he is going."

"Someone who doesn't know where they are, or where they have been, cannot know where they are going," Yore countered.

"But *I* know where they are going," said Yet. "I am the future. They are always going to me."

All of a sudden Yore became angrier than I had ever

seen him. He strode right up to Yet and jabbed his finger into the Future's flacid flesh.

"You," he said, "are an impostor. I have had enough of your artificial lies. I am fed up with the false pessimism of Tweedle Doom and the false optimism of Tweedle E. In the name of realism which steers a path between the two falsehoods, I exorcise you!"

"Not exercise!" Yet sneered sarcastically. "Anything but exercise. It's so exhausting. So barbaric. *So* old fashioned."

"And what is more," Yore continued, ignoring his adversary's ridicule, "I am about to call your bluff. You don't exist. Or at least you are not who you say you are. You are misnamed. You are not so much Yet as Yeti, the Abominable No Man!"

There was an awkward silence and I could see that Yet was extremely angry. His colour changed from bright electric blue, to a dull, throbbing claret. Tweedle E had become Tweedle Doom. His face appeared transfigured. Madly manic.

"No Future," he snarled, punk-like.

I found myself deeply alarmed at the transformation and looked across to Yo! for reassurance. He was staring at the apparition, apparently as horrified as I. Yore, however, stood his ground, dwarfed by the throbbing figure in front of him but refusing to give an inch. I admired his courage.

Yet had become an abomination and I hoped desperately that the ground would swallow him up as it had done so many times before.

At that moment, Yet changed again. The snarl sneered and then smiled. Then it began to laugh. The blob became blue again and immediately started to expand. The louder it laughed the larger it got. It laughed louder and louder and got larger and larger until it was a luminous blue globe, two hundred feet across.

I began to panic, as did Yo!, and we clasped each other tightly, looking on in horror as the bloated blob filled the sky. By contrast, Yore stood exactly where he had been, hands on elbows, solid jaw jutting forward in a gesture of defiance.

As the blob expanded it became more and more translucent, like a balloon.

"My God!" I screamed. "It's going to explode!"

Yo! and I dived for cover in the ditch.

Looking up I saw the blob grow larger and larger. Any moment now!

Phut. Bursting as harmlessly and silently as a bubble, it was gone. All that remained was the black-clad figure of Yore, standing alone in the field, staring at what remained. Empty space. Slowly, Yo! and I crawled from the ditch and joined him.

It was then that I noticed the change in Yo!. Moments before he had been wearing brightly coloured designer clothes. But now his garments, though still the same design, had lost all their colour. They were as black as coal. Yo! noticed the change at the same time and looked at himself in bewildered despair.

Yore smiled and held out his hand. "Welcome to the past!"

"The past?" Yo! puzzled, taking Yore's hand with a feeble uncertainty.

"Yes," Yore replied, "it happens to us all in the end."

"You mean I am no longer the present?"

"No, you are no longer the present. You are the recent past. There is a new present now."

"A new present?"

"Yes, the present is always new. Always impatient. It waits for no-one."

"So what's to become of me?"

Yore smiled. "This is only the end of the beginning for you."

"End of the beginning?"

"Yes, I shall show you. I'll be your guide in the journey from time to eternity."

"And what about me?" I asked feebly.
"Yo!" whispered Yo! sadly.
"It's goodbye for the time being," said Yore, stepping forward and hugging me warmly.
"For the time being?"
"Yes, while time is being we shall not meet again."
For the second time my eyes filled with tears.
"When?" I pleaded.
"Then," Yore replied, raising his hand with a finality forbidding further questions.

I shook his hand again, embraced him and then did the same with Yo! Finally, arm in arm, they strolled slowly eastward back into Sussex. Utterly alone, I watched as the two figures faded from space to wherever. I turned and followed the sunset into No-Man's Land.

The Saint Austin Press' Titles

A VICTORIAN CONVERT QUINTET
Rev. Michael Clifton
In this fascinating study of the faith journeys of five converts to Catholicism from the Oxford Movement, Fr. Michael Clifton invites the reader to consider the lessons we might learn from this *Quintet* of learned men.
212 pages, paperback, £9.95, ISBN 1-901157-03-2

DARKNESS VISIBLE
A Christian Appraisal of Freemasonry
Rev. Walton Hannah
Addresses the question of whether involvement with Freemasonry is compatible with one's duty as a practising Christian. It includes the entire and authentic text of the Masonic ritual of the first three degrees and of the Royal Arch.
232 pages, paperback, £12.95, ISBN 1-901157-709

AUGUSTINE OF CANTERBURY
Margaret Deanesly
This study deals with St. Augustine's training, character and background; the origins of his mission; his work in Kent; the structure of the church he established; the nature of the ministry he founded for the continuance of his work.
175 pages, paperback, £12.95, ISBN 1-901157-25-3

CATENA AUREA
A Commentary on the Four Gospels
St. Thomas Aquinas
Drawing completely on the Church Fathers, St. Thomas provides an indispensable verse by verse commentary on the Gospels. Translated under Cardinal Newman, introduced by Aidan Nichols OP.
2,825 pages, hardback, 4-volume set, £85,
ISBN 1-901157-40-7

The Saint Austin Press' Titles

POVERTY MY RICHES
A Life of St. Elizabeth of Hungary
Sr Elizabeth Ruth Obbard ODC
An inspiring account of the thirteenth-century wife, mother and queen who endured suffering all her life and died among the poor and sick whom she loved so much. A woman's account of this life of extraordinary sanctity.
106 pages, paperback, £9.95, ISBN 1-901157-80-6

THE VENERATION AND ADMINISTRATION OF THE EUCHARIST
The Proceedings of the 1996 Second International Colloquium on the Liturgy, organised by the Centre International d'Études Liturgiques (CIEL). Includes papers from leading theologians and explores aspects of the traditional Latin liturgy and the development of the Church's Eucharistic teaching.
255 pages, paperback, £12.95, ISBN 1-901157-15-6

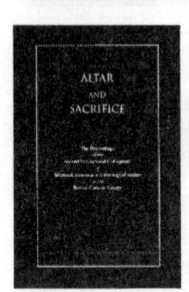

ALTAR AND SACRIFICE
The Proceedings of the 1997 Third International Colloquium of historical, canonical and theological studies on the Roman Catholic Liturgy, organised by the Centre International d'Études Liturgiques (CIEL).
An inspirational and fascinating collection of academic papers on the traditional Roman Liturgy given by international experts.
192 pages, paperback, £12.95, ISBN 1-901157-85-7

A BITTER TRIAL
Evelyn Waugh and John Carmel Cardinal Heenan on the Liturgical Changes
(Ed. Scott M. P. Reid)
For the last decade of his life, Waugh experienced the changes being made to the Church's liturgy as "a bitter trial." In Heenan he found a sympathetic pastor and kindred spirit. This volume contains the previously unpublished correspondence between these prominent Catholics, revealing in both an incisive disquiet.
71 pages, paperback, £3.95, ISBN 1-901157-05-9

The Saint Austin Press' Titles

THE CATHOLICISM OF SHAKESPEARE'S PLAYS
Peter Milward, S.J.
The local tradition in Stratford is that Shakespeare "died a Papist." Professor Peter Milward, of Sophia University, Tokyo, argues that the whole of Shakespeare's work reveals a common thread of sympathy with the plight of persecuted Catholics under Queen Elizabeth and King James I.
144 pages, paperback, £7.95, ISBN 1-901157-10-5

THE EARLY PAPACY
to the Council of Chalcedon in 451
Adrian Fortescue
A clear exposition and sound defence of the belief in the role of the Pope in the Church, drawing upon evidence from the Church Fathers up to 451 AD:

96 pages, paperback, £7.95, ISBN 1-901157-60-1

NEWMAN'S MARIOLOGY
Michael Perrott
A study of the development of Newman's beliefs about Our Lady, from the staid "Anglican red-letter days" of his time in Littlemore to the intimate and inspiring poetry of "The Dream of Gerontius" and his "Meditations and Devotions." Scholarly but immensely readable.
104 pages, paperback, £8.95, ISBN 1-901157-45-8

THE SIMPLICITY OF THE WEST
Peter Milward, S.J.
This work charts the idea of simplicity - as seen in the context of nature and tradition - through Socrates, St. Francis, St. Thomas Aquinas, to the present day. An exhilarating tour of Christian civilization with a profound message.
95 pages, paperback, £9.95, ISBN 1-901157-95-4

The Saint Austin Press' Titles

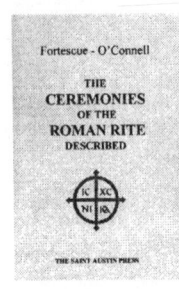

THE CEREMONIES OF THE ROMAN RITE DESCRIBED
Adrian Fortescue & J.B. O'Connell
A reprint of the 1962 edition of this classic ceremonial manual for the traditional Latin Mass. Published to support the work of the new traditional religious communities in union with the Holy See.

424 pages, hardback, £24.95, ISBN 1-901157-00-8

GENERAL SACRAMENTAL ABSOLUTION
Scott M. P. Reid
In this scholarly account, Reid argues that the use of General Absolution is not an appropriate response to the decline in confessions. A wide-ranging historical, canonical and pastoral perspective.
40 pages, paperback - stapled, £1.95
ISBN 1-901157-65-2

THE FACE OF THE NAZARENE
Noel Trimming
This dramatic and involving story is also a profound meditation on the Lord of the Millennia; Jesus Christ, the same yesterday, today and forever. It charts the impact of Christ on some of the people who knew him, in the hectic circumstances of their everyday lives.
157 pages, paperback, £9.95, ISBN 1-901157-90-3

LIFE OF ST. EDWARD THE CONFESOR
St. Aelred of Rievaulx
Translated into English for the first time by Fr Jerome Bertram, FSA. St. Edward built Westminster Abbey and was a great friend of the poor. An inspiring account of the life and miracles of England's Saintly King.
138 pages, paperback, £9.95, ISBN 1-901157-75-X

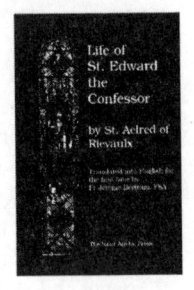

LEE COUNTY LIBRARY
107 Hawkins Ave.
Sanford, NC 27330